MALICIOUS PRINCE

BOOK THREE IN THE TERRITORIAL MATES SERIES

MARY E. TWOMEY

For my sister, Michelle.

For living and loving on your own terms.
For being brave, even when you're scared.

TWO PINPRICKS

SALEM

Traveling like this is the worst. Forget the fact tha we've got the handicap of a vampire with us, who can only travel by night. Push aside tha Des is moving at half his normal speed, due to recovering from the immense blood loss from his silver injury. Forget tha we're traveling with the bound and conked out General Klein—a decorated and trusted arsehole who tried to kill Des, Alex, me, a whole slew of fae, and his own daughter— twice. Ignore tha half of our party are not welcome in fae territory. It's the silence tha's killing me. All tha other stuff I could figure out, but Lily's lips haven't opened since Alex decided he couldn't live with her deadly abilities. I'm not sure if the tipping point for him was tha she kept it from us for so long, or if it's tha she can only produce plants tha harm or kill. Either way, I never thought I'd see Alex take himself out of the equation. Whenever Lily's around him, he brightens and softens and does all the things a lad in love does.

He'll come around.

"I can't," Des admits, holding up his left hand for us to stop. "I have to sit down."

"We've only been walking two hours. We have to make the most of the moonlight," I remind him. It's not like Des to ask for a break, so I know he's more injured than he's let on.

His breath comes out shallow, but his accent is perfectly proper, like always. "I lost too much blood. I'm not… I hate to be the one to bring up the fact that I'm a vampire, but, well, I'm a vampire, and I can't go this long fresh off an injury without blood to get me through. I don't know where to stop to refuel in this part of the world. I didn't pack extra blood because I was planning on us going back to the fae palace after I unlocked the gate to the Stone Graveyard and let you all out."

I tighten the reins of the horse I'm walking. The poor brown beast has the snoozing General Klein draped over its back. Lily bloomed a flower to keep him dozing, and tucked it in his lapel. "I can't even guess at where we might be able to get ye some filtered blood in fae territory."

Des swipes his left arm across his forehead to mop up the sweat. Faveda is tropical, but Des' perspiration doesn't look like it's from heat. He's fighting an infection. And losing. His right arm still hasn't been able to move, and it's been two days since we set off from the Stone Graveyard where we'd been trapped. We were trying to heal Faveda, and succeeded in ridding the land of the Gorgonell tha's been turning their people to stone. One would think tha would grant us a parade or at least a carriage to safe lodging, but tha's not how it's shaking out for us.

Good riddance.

Lily's been so silent tha her presence seems to fade into the background, though because we're mated, I'm still aware of every breath she takes. She's in agony, losing Alex to his anger, and there's no talking her out of punishing herself. She's not ready to speak yet, but she glides over to Des, who's given up on standing.

I have no idea what to do for him, other than keep him moving. "Let's go. The longer it takes for us to reach shelter, the worse this is going to get."

Des glowers up at me.

I'm not wrong. I mean, it's not like it's going to get easier for him to travel when there's even less blood in his belly eight hours from now. "I'm already at worse, Salem. Vampires can't live as long without blood as you all can go without food. And I'm coming off a silver injury, which no vampire's ever survived. I'm telling you, I'm desperate to drink, or I'm as good as dead out here."

I tilt my face skyward, asking the stars for any kind of guidance. Anything at all. "What do ye want me to do?"

Lily kneels in front of Des and tugs at her shirt collar, her eyes down and to the side as she offers him...

My stomach tightens in warning as Des' eyes soften. "I can't drink from you, blue eyes. The blood vampires drink has to be filtered. You know how it goes, yeah? Vampires drink filtered fae blood just fine, but not directly from the fae. In a pinch, I can drink directly from another vampire, but it looks like I'm the only one of me in fae territory." When Lily offers her neck again, Des places his hand on hers. "I'll only get sicker if I drink from someone who's got Green Lightning in their system. All fae are guarded against direct vampire feedings when they take Green Lightning. It was a nice thought, though."

She shakes her head, tugging at her collar again in offering.

I don't like this. I really don't like this.

Des' eyebrows raise. "Are you telling me you don't have Green Lightning in you? You didn't get a booster at the palace?"

Another shake of her head. Another reminder tha I haven't heard my mate's voice in days. I'm on the edge of imbalanced with her locked in this depression. I don't have the cruelty to try to pull her out of it. Her life is pretty grim right now. To try and cheer her up would be insulting and ineffective. Her father tried to kill her—once when she was a wee lass, and again two days ago. Her fae husband left her in the same month they married. She's in a country tha's supposed to be her homeland, but not a stitch of grass anywhere is familiar to her. And I bet she's waiting on us to leave her next, which I've tried to assure her isn't going to happen. But I guess tha's not the kind of thing ye can tell a woman; she has to see it practiced—daily staying with her and reminding her I'm not going anywhere.

"No," I finally work out. My throat is parched, and I

hope I'm hallucinating what I can't be seeing. "Ye can't let him drink from ye, pup." My attention switches to Des, who's sweat through his shirt and looks paler than a person has a right to be. "I would offer my blood, Brother, but everyone knows shifters can't sustain vampires."

Des' voice comes out cautious. "Lily, you should be on Green Lightning. That's so dangerous."

She shrugs. My mate shrugs tha she's not on the one thing tha keeps her from being attacked and exsanguinated by a vampire. Then again, maybe she missed her booster because we were expecting to go back to the palace, but ended up heading in the opposite direction. Still, my gut twists at the very illegal thing they should not be entertaining.

But Des won't make it to Jacoba without blood. My best mate will die if he doesn't feed soon. Everything in me is at war, so I stand stock-still with my fists clenched. We all know this is the only option, and it might not even work. The blood's supposed to be filtered. But it's our only shot, so I chew on my lower lip and let Lily look after my best friend in the way only she can.

Des takes her hand with trepidation. "I've never fed directly from a person before. It's not exactly something vampires are allowed to do. We don't even have the opportunity, as you're all on Green Lightning. Animals, sure, but not people. Are you certain you're okay with this?"

Worry creases her brow, but she bites down on her lower lip and nods, still unable to make eye contact.

I don't like this. We haven't seen a single home, person

or animal for miles, otherwise I'd bang on the door of the nearest fae for help, or hunt up some game for him to drain. The prairie has been stretching on for too long if it's led us to this fate.

I can see Des' relief before he takes a single drink. "Thank you. Thank you, Lily. I wouldn't even consider it if I wasn't on the brink of... Thank you. I'll do my best to be gentle. You have to tell me if I'm hurting you."

I hate everything about this. I tie the horse's reins to the nearest tree, giving him a few pats on his long flank for doing the deed of toting around the passed-out General. Then I make my way over to the two, doing what I can to talk myself out of intervening.

I'm hovering. I know it, but neither Lily nor Des calls me on it. The thought of Lily being feasted on by a vampire goes against everything in me. But the very real prospect of Des dying in my arms muddies my determination tha no harm should ever come near my mate.

"I'm sorry," Des murmurs, looking up at me with guilt in his eyes. "I didn't mean for this to happen. I already consumed my emergency supply of dried blood yesterday."

"No," I rule, though as I give my edict, I'm not sure I'm right. In fact, I'm certain I'm wrong to keep Des from sustenance tha comes to him voluntarily. "Ye can't drink from her. An open wound while we're on the road? She could get an infection. If she's weakened from too much blood loss, then what?"

Her body will make more, ye hovering baby. I know I'm being irrational, but I can't sit back and do nothing. What if Des does it wrong? He just said he's never fed from a person before. What if he really hurts her? Breaks a vein she needs tha won't easily repair? Then what?

It's Lily's hand on my arm tha stills the churning in my gut. It's not exactly words, but she's communicating nonetheless. The chaos in my chest settles by degrees. I take in the determination in her eyes tha trumps her fear, but doesn't erase it completely. Her eyes tell me to go, to spare me the sight of what I know I don't want to see.

If she wants me to leave when she might be in danger, she'll have to order me away, which we both know she's too depressed to do right now.

So I stay. My hands help her lay on the grass, making sure to choose the thickest, softest patch. Though, to be fair, all grass in Faveda is soft enough to be a pillow to cradle weary heads. Nature-affinity beings are spoiled by their surroundings. It's no wonder they're not bothered by the problems of the rest of the world.

I take Lily's lavender hair in my fist and twist it away from her neck, so Des doesn't pick the wrong vein by mistake. Stinking moonlight. There's barely enough light to see anything.

Now I'm sweating, pursing my lips through panic tha churns like vomit in my gut. I'm trying to keep my cool, but it's a bad act. When Des lays next to her, barely able to prop himself up with his one good arm, I'm unable to curb the anxiety tha spills from my lips. "Careful, Des. Just enough to keep ye going, not more than tha. You're going to hurt her. Don't bite too hard. But if it's not hard enough, ye might tear more things. Precision. Quick and painless, aye?"

Jays, I sound annoying, even to myself, but I don't care. I care tha Lily is safe.

Lily looks dead to the world as she lays on her back, the fire in her blue eyes dulling to a blasé "I guess this is my life now," kind of vacant stare up at the stars. I can't stand to see her like this. A fresh wave of fury comes over me, and I fight down the urge to beat her da into an early grave. He deserves it for all he's done to her.

Patience. Lily hasn't lived in a land with laws in a long time. If she's going to rule, she'll need to, well, abide by the rules. Murder isn't the best choice when imprisonment is an option.

Though it is tempting.

Des opens his mouth over the juncture between her neck and shoulder, but pauses and frowns up at me when a whine of terror leaks from between my lips. "You're making me even more nervous, Salem. Seriously, I love her just as much as you do, mate. I don't *want* to do this. I *have* to, and you hovering like this is only making things worse."

He's right, but I can't hold myself back. "I know, but I can't leave. Do your thing, just make it quick. This is as calm as I get when a vampire's about to suck the life out of the lass I love."

Des' jaw tightens. "I love her, too, you know. I know this mate bond is new, and it's messing with everything inside of you right now, but you have to see me, too. I *have* to live through this if we're going to unite the territories."

He looks down at her innocent face, and then presses his nose into her cheek, inhaling the sweet scent of her creamy skin. Maybe some people might argue the three claw marks across the side of her face are flaws. Those people are stupid, and I'll cheerfully beat them to a bloody pulp for saying anything bad about my mate. Des kisses her cheek with a sadness I feel deep in my bones. "She's my wife, Salem. I'll be careful."

Being mated to my best friends' wife isn't easy, but we've been managing thus far. I'm making things worse than they have to be, but I can't stop myself.

"I'm not even sure this will work." Des touches his lips to the shell of her ear and whispers, "Thank you for letting me try."

Then, before I can give him five more reasons why he can't do this to her, Des opens his mouth and bites down on tha tender spot in the curve on the side of her neck. A soft gasp flies from her lips in time with her eyes widening, taking in the full expanse of the starry sky. Her eyes flick from side to side as breath comes in ragged pants and rough bursts. She's been mute and despondent for days, but now her hips move against the night air like she's trying to get some satisfaction through the layer of denim. Her fingers tangle in his hair and tug. I'm ready to intervene if it looks like she's trying to push him away, but she doesn't. She holds his face tighter to her neck, giving with more enthusiasm as her eyes roll back with something tha can't be anything other than pleasure.

The waves of her hips and her blood are coaxing sexual

moans from my best friend, who swallows with his eyes shut tight, like he's in the best kind of pain. He undulates against her side, goading her on. It's carnal and strange, and the first sign of life she's exhibited in days.

My heart is breaking, like the whole of me might be in full cardiac distress. I don't like any man near her, and though I understand Des belongs to her, so do I. I guess I haven't reconciled her marriages as much as I'd thought. It's an ocean of confusion, wanting Des to live and also wanting to tear his head off. I'm shaking. My whole body is vibrating with two very different urges.

I want to pull him off of her, but just before I'm ready to yank him back, Des rolls to the side, a trail of blood dotting his cheek as he touches his belly, finally sated.

In the next breath, I've got Lily gathered up in my arms. I run her away from the General, away from Des, and away from the visual I never want to endure again. She's limp in my arms when I finally stop running. I slump with my back against a tree, terrified and horrified. I don't like to part with the napkins she gave me on my visits to her pub. I know it's pathetic to keep mementos of something tha was so very nothing, but every word she said to me back when she was my waitress is precious, so I wrote it down. Every interaction for five years has a napkin dedicated to it, with my penmanship spelling out each word she spoke to me. Most of them are in my safe back home, but I keep a stash on me in my breast pocket at all times, ensuring she's close to my heart.

As I take one out and use it to blot the two puncture

wounds on her neck, my tight scrawl stares up at me as it quickly stains with her blood. *"Here's your usual, Prince Salem. Can I get you anything else tonight?"* The memory of Lily with her lavender curls bound up atop her head and her waitress apron draped across her hips smacks me across the face. I don't want to forget tha moment, tha span of time before I pushed her to marry my best friends. I don't regret the path we're on, but I also loathe its necessity. I didn't think I had a shot with her, and now this perfect creature is my mate.

My mate tha's bleeding in my arms.

"I'm sorry," I plead. "I shouldn't have let Des do tha. The blood's clotting okay, but it was all wrong. I'm sorry!"

Lily still doesn't speak; she merely lifts her hand to touch my cheek, looking into my eyes with the briefest brush of clarity breaking through her haze. I want her to speak to me, even if it's to cuss me out. But she's not ready, so she gives me tha small touch before she slips back into her oblivion.

I bury my sins and my nose in her cheek, promising I'll give her a better life than this. I rock us both, forward and back. I'm buried in untold amounts of pain because of those two small pinpricks on her neck.

Damn ye, Alex. Ye did this to her.

2

MY MATE'S BLOOD

SALEM

The enclosed carriage I rented the second we crossed over onto shifter soil is the best use of thirty coins I can think of. I let the fae horse go in Faveda, and bound the drooling General atop the cart, high enough for shifters not to take bites out of him. Lily still hasn't spoken, but now tha her da's out of her sight, she closes her eyes. I tuck a gray wool blanket around her tha I bought for another five coins. I don't like her pallor, even less when she shivers. I know fae aren't built for the harsher shifter winters, but it's barely autumn, so I'm hoping she doesn't fall ill before we reach the safety of the mansion.

She relaxes against Des, who wears a second blanket over his head to cover himself in case the doors are flung open for any reason. He's stronger, far more himself, now tha he's got her blood in him. But his right arm is still dead from where General Klein stabbed him with the silver blade. I don't know what to do about it, other than get him to a healer as soon as we get home. The sun is starting to rise, so I take care to make sure the curtains are drawn and nothing can harm my best friend.

"Don't bite her," I warn for the sixth time in the past two hours. "I'll be driving, so I can't keep an eye on things."

Des is a good enough lad not to be insulted. He lifts the edge of the blanket to peek out at me. "Of course. I won't feed on her unless you're there. It matters to me that she's alright, too, Salem."

"I know. I just…" I can't explain it, and luckily, Des doesn't make me. He grants me half a smile as he coils his good arm around Lily, holding her tight to his side when it seems she's determined to drift off into her depression. Then he covers both their heads with the blanket. Though she doesn't need to be shaded from the sunlight, I know Des wants her as close as possible. Being near her is an addiction we've both accepted is impossible to kick.

I shut the door, wishing it could be me holding her, and take my spot as the coachman. I know Alex and Des would've hired a person to drive them, but tha's just not me. If something needs doing tha I can take care of, I do it myself. I'm not big into trust, and it takes too much of the stuff for me to hand over the reins to anyone. Especially now tha my mate's in the carriage. If she needs to be driven somewhere, *I'll* be holding the reins. *I'll* lock the door for her. *I'll* make sure she doesn't get too cold.

I'm the worst, but Lily doesn't show her impatience with me when I have to stop the carriage every hour all day long. I make sure we're covered in shade, of course, and I check to make sure no one's around so they aren't tipped off to the precious cargo I'm driving around, but I know she's probably annoyed tha I keep checking on her.

"We're really okay, Salem," Des assures me with a wry smile, his arm still affixed around her shoulders while she stares vacantly out the shaded window. "You know I'll call up to you if we need something."

"Yeah, yeah." The truth is it's *me* who's not okay. It's too long since I've held her. Too many days since she's smiled at me. No one smiles at me except the lads. But she does. She makes me want to be the kind of person who cracks jokes and says clever things, like Alex and Des do. Though I know she won't answer, I speak to her all the same. "Lily, I'm going in to get some lunch for us. Anything ye want?"

She shrugs, which is almost like talking but not quite.

"Prince Salem? It's Prince Salem!" someone shouts from behind me. I shut the door quickly, on edge until I hear Des click the lock from the inside.

I nod to the lad announcing my presence. I don't recognize him, but tha's not all too uncommon. He's younger than military age, so he's of little use to me yet.

"Prince Salem, we've been waiting for your return! Are ye going to have the troops fix the fallen section of the border?"

I quirk my eyebrow, which is the most I'll converse about the subject I know nothing of.

The teenager with freckles and ruddy cheeks points westward. "Parts of it were knocked over, and no one's fixed it yet. There's some worry tha the fae will try to sneak across into our land and steal our plumapples."

Of all the things to worry about. I want to tell him to let the fae take what healing apples they need, but tha's a thing I should probably tell my soldiers first. "Aye," I tell the lad, whose chest puffs tha he delivered important news. He'll make a grand soldier someday—eager to please and loyal to the throne. "I don't suppose I could give you some coin to go in and buy us some food."

His rust-colored eyebrows shoot up into his hairline as his pitch climbs. "Of course! My da owns the store. Whatever ye fancy, I'll fetch it for ye. No charge for the throne."

I give him a nod, but shove a handful of coins into his fist. I'm not in the business of taking things from my people. They pay taxes already; they've no need to pay more. "Some fruit and nuts." I'm dying for a tall stein of ale, but I can't let my guard down until Lily's safe in my home. In my bed. I need to change those sheets. "Another blanket. A tin of fish and some bread." Lily might be pale; it's hard to tell when she's tucked in the shade of the carriage. "Iron pills, if your da has them."

"Aye, your majesty. Right away!" His eyes glance up at the tarp I've used to cover General Klein's body. "Fresh kill?"

"Prisoner," I correct him, giving him the subtle hint to hurry.

It does the trick, because he scampers away toward the general store.

"The lad's either too young or too stupid to catch tha

your prisoner's fae," says a voice from the other side of the carriage.

Grand.

I loathe the members of the cabinet who think they know how the territory should be run, and whine when they don't get their way. Sir Muttrend points a gnarled finger to the General's hand sticking out the side of the tarp, revealing pale skin and a pure white sleeve.

"Go on, Mutt," I tell him, tucking the General's hand back under the covering. "It's no business of yours."

"Sir Muttrend," he corrects me, though I don't know why he bothers. I'm never going to use his full name when "Mutt" is such a grand nickname for a man who is constantly pushing for purebred pairings and frowning on those shifters with differing animals who intermarry. As if we have the means, time or desire to enforce something like tha.

His chubby fingers pass over the tarp and land on the dark wood of the carriage. Though I'm taller than him, he somehow manages to look down his long, hooked nose at me. "When I heard Prince Salem procured a carriage at the border, I had to see for myself what ye were hauling. It's not every day the prince comes to us by way of Faveda, of all places. Ye usually come back from your travels via Neutral Territory."

"How grand tha ye have so much free time tha ye check up on me. I'll have to tell Justice to give ye and the rest of the cabinet more to do."

He tsks me, as if he's the one in charge. Like the fact tha

he's old means he can scold me. "Now, now. No need to get foul. I'm just sad no one's helped ye with your cargo." He bares his canines, his snarl affixed on the General.

"Are the jail cells full?" I ask, tightening the ropes tha hold the tarp in place.

He scratches his portly belly. "Of course not. Your brother is too lenient. There are many who deserved to be locked up tha walk free. We can start with the judges who perform the marriages of mixed-breed couplings."

I'm so tired of his needling. I almost want to let it drop tha I've not only mated outside my breed, but outside my race as well. But this hardly seems the time. Should probably tell my brother first. "A wolf shifter has every right to breed with a bear shifter, a dog, a cat or whomever. Concern yourself with the drought, not what merriment people do to forget their woes."

"Tha wasn't your da's rule."

Mutt's a foul arse. "My da is dead, and so are the old ways. Your proposal to outlaw cross-breed marriages was overruled. Deal with it. Justice will hear of ye speaking out against his laws when I get home."

Mutt holds up his hands. "Is free speech suddenly outlawed?"

I step toward him, and I can see his eyes once again measuring his prowess to my muscle. A man in his sixties has no business taking on a prince in his prime, so Mutt's constantly using his best weapon—his words. Justice should take him off the cabinet, but out of respect to Da, who appointed the idiot, he doesn't. "Go about your business, Mutt, and leave me to mine. You'll do well to never speak poorly of my brother or my da in my presence."

I don't like Mutt sniffing around my carriage.

"Who's inside? More fae prisoners? I'm picking up a strong hint of fae, and I can't imagine it's all coming from your prisoner up top."

I'm sure Des and Lily are completely motionless inside, but it's easy to catch the aroma of a fae. They give off this floral scent tha's hard to ignore.

Mutt's pudgy fingers on the handle is the last straw.

I shift before I can talk myself out of it. I know it's a bad move, but I can't hold back. It's a clear act of aggression, which never goes over well.

Mutt smiles, taking my challenge as permission to be as ruthless as he pleases. He jumps up and transforms into his panther, tearing at the tarp and digging a long scratch down General Klein's leg. Mutt doesn't attack me; he knows tha would get him thrown in jail.

This is lawlessness. This is a man who advises the throne but doesn't respect it.

I chase him, running after the flailing tarp and growling to let him know I'm not letting this go. Bristly trees whip by us, the unending greens of Faveda long gone. Every bit of nature is vastly browner the further into Jacoba ye travel.

The mangey codger darts in between bushes far more gracefully than I ever could with speed tha most envy. But he should know better than to taunt me. I'm hot on his heels, and pounce, sinking my teeth into the scruff of his neck and shaking until the tarp breaks free. I don't even care about the tarp. It's being stolen from in any way tha gets under my skin. If the cabinet thinks they can take an inch of anything from me, they'll walk all over me, like they try to do to Justice.

I don't hold back as I tear into Mutt's flesh, tasting the tang of his blood before I fling him free. He lands on all fours with a mewl, the stupid cat, but he limps away with a threat on his lips.

Mutt's got triumph in his eyes, even as he limps away to lick his wounds. I have no idea what he's got to be smug about until I hear Des cry out through the forest-lined expanse. "Salem, help!"

Lightning zips through my body, turning me on my heels as I charge toward the carriage. *A diversion,* I cringe, cursing myself as I run with panic fueling my pace. I'm faster on four legs but I'm bigger on two, so I run my heart out in my wolf form, grateful I didn't stray too far. I howl, hoping to alert everyone tha I'm on my way. My howl should rally the hearts of my beloveds, and strike terror into the souls of my enemies.

I'm not the only one who hears Des' cry for help. I rally when I catch sight of a few wolves in the distance perking up at the sound of my call. They run in the direction of danger, not away from it, howling to let me know I'm not on my own. While I don't give a rat's arse if different breeds intermarry, there's solidarity tha's found among a shifter's own kind. The wolves don't need to know the ins and outs of my plight; they understand one of their own needs them, so they come.

There will always be those who challenge the throne, and there will always be those who defend it.

I leap in through the carriage door tha looks splintered open, and sink my canines into the second panther tha's making a mess of things with a pit bull.

I can't deal with the eagle who's picking at the General yet, because Des is in real danger. I know it wounds him to leave the fighting to Lily while he cowers inside their blankets to keep from the sunlight.

Lily's boot kicks at the pit bull's flat-faced mug, but the thing keeps coming back for her, even after I'm dragging the panther out of the carriage and shaking it until it can't stand on its own. It'll heal, though hopefully with more sense in his head next time around. I focus my mind and send a message to the overgrown cat. *"A swift beating's the only thing you'll earn when ye follow Sir Muttrend rather than the throne. If I see your gob again, I'll have your tail."*

The sound of Lily's pain pierces my ears, my heart and several other things I need to survive. I don't hesitate when I barrel into the carriage again, still ignoring the eagle who's going to town on the General. I don't bother with a growl of warning; the lad saw the carriage was mine before he decided to attack. He's got his teeth buried in Lily's calf, and doesn't let go until I close my jaw around his throat.

The pit bull releases her with a yowl of pain. I only catch a whiff of her blood before I've pummeled him clear out of the carriage.

Lily closes the door behind me to keep the sun from Des. Tha's my girl. Always protecting. Always thinking. I lock the image of her fright in my mind as I tear out the throat of the pit bull, knowing I'm going against my own belief I've been trying to instill in Lily. This shifter needs to be in prison, not in the ground, but I can't stop. I'm hungry for his blood now. I can see her crimson on his teeth, and I can't hold back. He hurt Lily. He made my mate scream. My rage kicks into high gear, and before I know it, the vicious fleabag is motionless under my paws.

I can't stop. My body doesn't know how. I need to know my mate is safe, so I rip the flesh from his bones and fling the strips over my shoulder. My heart is pounding, my breath coming in pants and bursts as I try to talk myself down from my rage.

The other wolves finally join me, but back up when they see me mid-rage. They send me messages of support and caution, asking me if I'm alright, and how they can help.

I might be beyond help, so gone am I for Lily.

"Guard the carriage," I tell them through our shifter connection. *"Sir Muttrend organized this. If he comes sniffing around, he's not to get near."* They don't need to be asked twice. They're not even soldiers, just passersby who don't value looking the other way when help is needed. Tha's what I love about my people.

Most of them.

The eagle stills above me, and when I finally glance up

to growl at the bird, he takes off, abandoning his prey and zipping through the woods.

I'm on two legs somehow. I can't even remember shifting back, but I'm grunting through the trauma of nearly losing my mate.

Lily's arms are around me. When did she get out of the carriage? She's kissing my temple and coaxing me down from the adrenaline I haven't felt this sharply since… since she was in danger the last time. Only this is different, because we're in shifter territory. Anyone could come for her at any time with fangs sharpened and hungry eyes.

The wolves back down but don't leave, so shocked are they at the sight of a fae lass doting on a shifter. Her touch is so gentle tha it reminds me I must be careful if I'm to be near someone this incredible.

"You're bleeding," I croak, unwilling to address the thing I've just done. The thing I told her rulers can't do.

I've murdered one of my own. No trial, just swift vindication.

"I'm alright," she promises me. It's the first thing she's said in days, and I don't believe a word of it. "Let's get out of here."

She kisses my cheek, and I feel my chest expand in a more natural rhythm. My arms band around her, and I want to bury my shame in her hair. I just killed one of my kin. Not just a shifter, but a shifter from the same lineage as me. A fellow canine. I don't feel as much attachment to the feline family, though I would never kill one of them in my right mind, either.

I'm not in my right mind.

"I need to get home. I need to talk to my brother." Justice will be able to explain things. He'll know what to do. Maybe there's some way to calm me down, so I'm not on the edge of murder every time Lily's in the least bit of danger.

The lad I sent to fetch me the supplies stands a stone's throw away with the wolves, his freckles standing more prominently against his gaunt face. I'm not sure if he's more upset tha my coach was attacked, tha a dead shifter's innards are spilled on the grass, or tha a fae woman has her arms around my neck.

Lily helps me up, and I turn her so I can address the wolves. "Thanks for coming to my aid."

They bow, but I can hear snippets of their confusion. They certainly didn't mean to guard a fae from harm, but tha's what they did simply because I asked. Tha's loyalty.

Lily bows her head to them, not because they'll ever understand or accept her, but because she's good. Truly good deep down. "Thank you for rescuing Salem. You must be who he's talking about when he talks about how much he loves his people."

Of course she charms them with two sentences. Their mumbles of confusion turn to amusement and a tingle of respect before they meander away, leaving me to my mess.

Lily meets my eyes with unfathomable sadness and worry. "I don't know how to tell a good shifter from a bad one."

I take her hand and rest it on my heart. "The good ones

think about their neighbor. The bad ones think only of themselves. Same as fae."

"You're hurt," she remarks, her eyes moistening as if my pain pierces her worse than it does me.

"S'nothing."

She bites down on her lower lip, like she wants to argue but doesn't have it in her right now. Instead of staying by my side, she limps back into the carriage.

I hate the sight of the red ribbons streaking down her leg, but she doesn't complain. She simply tosses me a smile tha's supposed to reassure me, but in my heart, I know I'm to blame for this. My mate's blood is dotting the dirt of my homeland. I shouldn't have let Mutt distract me. I shouldn't have left her for the briefest of seconds. I won't make tha mistake again.

I take the supplies from the lad without a word, put them in the carriage, tie up the dead body next to the moaning and bleeding General on the roof, and heft myself back up onto the coachman's seat. With my head lowered, I crack the reins and take off toward the mansion.

3

VERA'S LOVE

DESTINO

Sunlight is the bloody worst. It takes us twice as long to get to Salem's mansion in Jacoba, since they've taken on the handicap of traveling with me. Probably would've been three times as long if he hadn't secured us the carriage. When I finally cross over the threshold, my exhale of relief comes out in a joyous cry that wakes the house. "Apologies," I say to the housekeeper who comes bounding around the corner. "Hallo, Vera. Did you miss me, lovely girl? Made it in here just before the sun rose."

Vera loathes me, so her snarl isn't unexpected. I don't know why her overt disdain always makes me smile, but despite being tired and thirsty, I chuckle as her messy gray curls swish around her round face when she shakes her head at me. "Wake me before the crack of dawn again, and I'll lock the doors when I see ye coming next. The sunlight seems like a good place for ye."

"You minx. Tell me how much you've missed me. It's

been ages. Has it really been a year? You poor thing. To have lived that long without my smile. Resilient thing, you are."

"How long are we stuck with ye this time?"

"That's up to Salem, but I think you'll have enough days and nights with me to get your fill of my face. You're so lucky."

"I'm already sick of your gob. Out ye go."

The door opens and shuts again, and Salem marches past us with Lily in his arms. The sight of her heats my insides and draws my eyes. Though she's been snuggled up to me for days, she's been too despondent for conversation.

"Ack! Prince Salem, what are ye doing with tha fae? Get her out!"

Salem growls at Vera, though how she could've known Lily belongs here now is anybody's guess. Still, Salem doesn't care about reason. He only cares for Lily, the brute. His snarl grows until Vera recoils. "Take a good look at this lass, Vera. This is Lilya Klein. She's going to live with me in the mansion, and I won't hear her disrespected in her own home."

"What?" Vera screeches, her jowls shaking with confusion and indignation. "Prince Salem, tha's enough nonsense! Take tha fae out of here right this instant!"

Vera's been with the family forever, and is probably the only person who can order around the Butcher boys with any real gusto.

But Vera doesn't know all that's changed in the boy she

raised, and her racist mouth's about to get her into more trouble than she can handle.

I push Salem toward the hallway before this gets any worse. "Take her to your room and get her settled in, brother." Then to Vera, I ask, "Vera, my lovely plum, could you call us a healer? My wife was attacked on our way here."

"Pity it wasn't *ye* some clever shifter took a bite out of."

Oh, Vera.

Salem leaves down the stone hallway with Lily, who's clinging to him with her face buried in his shirt.

Vera turns to leave, but stops short when my words sink in. "Wait, your wife? Who's your wife? Please don't tell me we'll be forced to provide lodging for ye *and* another vampire."

I give her my best fake laugh. "I wouldn't dream of it. That was my wife, just there. That luscious fae you saw in Salem's arms, who still needs you to call her a healer, by the way."

She blinks at me and chortles. "Ho, tha's a good one. Ye almost had me there. Go on up to your usual room and try not to burden us all with your peculiar blood habits. And Prince Salem better not be taking tha fae woman to his room."

Yes, my peculiar blood habits, like survival.

"The healer, Vera. I need you to call one, yeah? I'll wait."

She shakes her head at me. "To look at tha fae lass' leg? You'll have to pay a pretty coin to convince a shifter to treat a fae. To be honest, the healer who'll agree to look after a fae is one tha's probably not worth the paper his degree's been printed on."

Fair point. "My sweet, Vera. Are you ever not honest? Every word that slips from your lips is pure poetry."

I sit on the counter—a move that draws scandalized gasps in Faveda, but here earns me a swat from the dish towel. I love it. My own mum wouldn't pay me such attention if I lit myself on fire. Vera despises me, but it's our game. I'm fairly certain that she loves me. Beneath the venomous hatred, that is.

Vera grumbles at me and then shuffles toward the door, shoving her feet in her boots. "It's almost six in the morning, ye realize. I'm going out to fetch a healer for some fae woman at nearly six in the morning. The things I do for those boys."

We both know she has to hate me, but if it was just me who needed a healer, and not a random fae, she would do it. It would involve the same amount of grousing, but it would happen. I've known Vera since I was a boy, and while the old prejudices run deep, I was a very adorable child. "Sorry I kept Salem away longer than usual. It's been a bit busy, what with my wedding and all. Needed a best man."

She rolls her eyes. "Yes, your vampire marriage to a fae. Hilarious. Tell me, did a shifter officiate?"

"Actually, yes. A shifter from Neutral Territory." I smile at the memory of Lily and me huddled in Judge Pohl's dreary living room, signing papers and holding each other's hands while we made history by moonlight.

"Of course. Nice touch, adding in Neutral Territory. Ye kept my Salem away too long. Justice has been needing him. Gets lost if they're apart for too long. He's afraid to make any decisions without Salem here. I don't have it in me to sit back and say nothing."

"No, you? But you're so quiet and meek."

She scoffs. "Tell Salem he needs to stay for a while. There've been rumblings."

"Rumblings?"

She nods sagely. "Of fae trying to break through our borders to steal our plumapples. Can ye imagine? As if they don't have enough in life. Taking what's ours and giving nothing in return while our people are rationing out a cup of water."

I cross my legs as I get comfortable on the granite countertop. "What do you reason would be a fair trade for something like that?"

Her mouth draws to the side. "I wouldn't say no to a few more wells. The fae can shoot water out their arses. Ain't no reason they couldn't fill our wells. Make our land just as nice as theirs, selfish pricks."

I consider her wisdom, which always comes to the tune of criticism. Whenever Alex comes to visit, he refills their wells, but it doesn't last forever. They need maintenance, and Alex is being too much a brat to bother with us now.

Vera tosses her dishrag at me, but when I move to catch it with my dominant hand, my limb still doesn't obey. I try not to worry when I say "Oops" as it smacks off my chest and drops to the floor.

A frown puckers her lips, and then she throws a shoe that's resting near the back door at me. That one, I catch with my left hand, though I fumble a bit first.

"What's wrong with your right arm, lad?"

I swallow down my panic and don a confident smile that's seen me through many a hardship. "I guess I'm not infallible after all. I was stabbed on my way here."

Despite her insistence that I'd be better off dead, she stiffens. "Who's daft enough to attack the Prince of Drexdenberg?"

"A great many people, actually. Salem's got the offender in your prison. Dropped the lowlife off on our way here. The fae General shot me with a silver-tipped arrow."

She gasps and runs to me, not caring that she's tracking dried bits of dirt all over the stone floor. "What? Ye can't be serious. Ye would've died! How, Destino?"

I jump down and turn around, taking my shirt off to show her the entry point. "Anything to get my clothes off me, you old flirt. But I told you, I'm a married man."

Her fingers trace the tender spot that really shouldn't still be sore to the touch. Then again, by all logic, I should be dead. We're in uncharted territory, I guess, so I don't complain about it as she prods at the wounded area. "How?" she breathes, every bit as worried as I am.

"I'm not sure," I admit. I know it was Lily, but how she did it, I couldn't say. "I could really use that healer, after they finish looking at Lily."

"Who? Oh, tha fae woman. This is more important than

any fae taking ill with a broken nail or whatever it is tha troubles the delicate folk."

I turn my chin over my shoulder. "Be better than common, Vera. You know she was bloody and couldn't walk. She was injured enough to scare Salem, and you should care about what scares your prince." Though, to be fair, if Lily sneezed twice, I'm fairly certain Salem would be just as finicky.

"Scolding me, are ye?"

I reach behind me with my left and hold onto her hand —a thing I only do when no one's around to catch her being kind to me. "Find that healer, Vera. I'm alive, but I don't have any feeling in my right arm at all. Can't move my fingers. Can't lift my wrist. Nothing. If that's the trade I have to make for keeping my life, so be it, but if it can be helped, I'd very much like to hold my wife with both arms, and rule my territory with my right hand as well."

Her eyebrows shoot up. "Since when are ye in line to rule? I thought tha ship sailed."

News often doesn't travel to the neighboring territories at all, since no one likes each other all that much. "King Ronin decreed it after he found out my father was poisoning him, trying to pollute his mind and get Ronin declared unfit to rule. Ronin retaliated by murdering Father right in front of me and the entire kingdom, and then announced that I would be taking the crown in a year's time with my new wife."

Vera clucks her tongue and shakes her head. "I'm not sure if congratulations are in order, but if they are, well, good for ye. Or would condolences be best? I'm not sure. Being responsible for a land of vampires seems like a life sentence, not a reward. Though, I am sorry ye had to see your da die, nasty prig though he was."

"I'm past the pain of it all," I lie.

"Aye, of course ye are. Heartless vamps, the whole lot of ye."

"Easy, Vera," I warn quietly, letting her know she's pouncing on my soft spots.

She pats my good arm. "Fine, fine. So who is she, this woman who's finally making an honest lad of ye? And don't start up with tha lie about her being fae. Tell me who she really is."

"Her name is Lily, and once you stop hating her, you'll love her." I can't keep the anxiety completely scrubbed from my voice. "Vera, hurry. We need that healer. Quick as you can."

"Aye. I'll see to it right now. And I won't settle for sub-par healers, neither. Only the best to look at your arm. They'll want to see this. A vampire surviving silver? Never thought I'd see the day. Whatever luck ye live by, pray to the clouds it never runs out."

As she crosses the room and pushes open the door, I follow her advice and hope for the best.

HEALED AND BROKEN

SALEM

I hate this. Letting another man touch my mate is torture on a good day, which this is not. At least Healer Wesley looks to be about sixty, and not interested in anything other than Lily's injuries. "Curious. Though, I've never treated a fae before, so perhaps this is normal."

"What?" I practically shout when he pauses in thought for too long.

My volume startles him, and I feel a wee bit guilty for putting everyone in the room on edge. Lily reaches up and strokes my arm. "Easy, pup," she soothes me as only she can.

Healer Wesley studies our touch with curiosity but doesn't address it. He seems wholly focused on her bite marks tha are tearing at my insides. I would never tell her, but my leg's been hurting in the same spot since about half an hour after she got bitten. I've heard of shifters taking ill when their mate gets sick, but I always kind of wrote most of it off as dramatics. But my leg aches when I walk now, so I know she's in pain.

"Now, I don't know enough about fae to tell ye what to do, so I'll only tell ye what I'd tell a shifter child. Best err on the safe side of things." Healer Wesley has rust-colored hair with gray wisps and a wide nose, which twitches whenever he excitedly stumbles upon a new facet of the mysterious fae. His eyeballs are overly round, so when he widens them at my manic volume, it looks like they might pop out of his head.

"That sounds okay. Go ahead and do what you need to. Salem's a little anxious, but you're a good guy, right?"

The question in her casual tone hits my nerves like a gong. She's scared of him, and not because he's a shifter. Well, not *just* because of tha. He has kindness in his eyes, and though I want to shove him across the room for touching her ankle like he knows her, part of me appreciates tha he's making an awkward situation not so hard. "When was the last time ye saw a Healer, lass?" he asks her.

"My mom was a shifter healer, so I guess all the time, though I haven't lived with her in a few months."

He quirks his eyebrow at her. "Ye have a shifter mammy?"

She nods. "I'm from Neutral Territory," she explains without explaining, and then sighs. "I don't really want to talk about it. How busted up is my leg? When can I run around on it?"

"You've got a few lacerations tha need stitches, but I

don't know what kind of thread and needle to use. Fae are so delicate. What did your mammy do for ye?"

She shrugs. "Same needle and thread she used to fix up the shifters and vamps who came to us for help."

I fight back a whine. "What sort of injuries has she had to stitch up on ye?"

She pats my cheek. "Easy, pup."

Des wanders in, and for a second, it all feels so normal —him checking up on us, Lily sitting on the chair in my room. "How's my bride?" he asks, claiming her in front of the healer more naturally than I'm able. I need to tell Justice first. I have loads of questions about all the ins and outs of being mated. Never paid much attention to the details before.

"I'm alright," Lily replies, gripping the arms of the chair as Healer Wesley pours alcohol over the wound.

She grits her teeth through her hiss of pain, and before I know it, I'm fisting the man's collar, kicking his legs out from beneath him and dragging him away from her.

"Salem, stop!" Lily cries, which is the only sound I listen to anymore.

I pause and turn, releasing the man with a mix of gruff chagrin. I don't know what my deal is. I know he's helping her. "He gave ye pain," I explain, sounding like an oaf.

Lily's patient with me, and luckily Des helps Healer Wesley to his feet and dusts him off. "Salem, you have to let him look at my leg. He's going to give me stitches, and it's not going to feel wonderful, but it's necessary." I see a decision click in her eyes. "Into the hallway with you."

"But I…"

She points to the door. "Des can stay with me, if you're worried about the healer going off-book. Just five minutes, pup."

Des pokes at the skin under her eyes. "She needs vitamin C. Can you get her some orange juice or something, Brother?"

I'm already out the door and jogging down the halls toward the kitchen.

I need to make it nicer in my bedroom. There's nothing but a bed, a chair, a desk and a chest of drawers for my clothes. It's a huge room, but it's never felt bare before today. And the kitchen needs to be stocked with her favorite things, not tha I know what they are. She likes baking those cookies, I know tha much.

I grab a bag of oranges from the hanging basket and set to work juicing. Everything is stone here—lots of grays. I never minded it before, but Lily just came from the ivorum palace where everything was bright and sparkling with cleanliness.

Justice trots into the kitchen, throwing his head back in relief at the sight of me. "Salem, Vera told me ye were home, but since ye didn't come say hello, I thought she must be telling tales. I missed ye, Brother." He claps me twice on the back of my shoulder.

"Aye," I grunt and keep juicing. "Good to be back."

"Where's Alexavier? The wells are dangerously low. Is tha where he's at now? I tell ye, if he wasn't fae, I'd kiss the bastard for bringing water back to our land on his visits."

I really don't want to talk about this. "Alex isn't here, and he's not coming to Jacoba for the foreseeable future."

Justice stills. "Don't tell me the unbreakable trio had a rumble. Never thought I'd see the day." Then he grips the counter's edge. "Ye can't mean he's not coming back at all, only tha we need to hold on a little while longer, right?"

"Alex isn't coming back, maybe ever. We'll have to find another way to get Jacoba some water."

Justice grips the ledge and slowly shakes his head. "No, Salem. Whatever it is, ye have to make it right. Our people will die if the water isn't replenished."

I grab for another orange and split it open, then grind it on the juicing wedge. "I brought General Klein to decorate our dungeon. Ye can put him to work, if ye like, though I'm not sure I'd drink a damn thing tha man makes."

Justice hangs his head. "Ye captured General Klein? Do ye think tha's wise? Isn't tha an act of war on the fae? What could he have possibly done tha we haven't done ten times over?"

I keep my eyes on the orange in my fist. "He shot Des with a silver-tipped arrow and tried to kill me, Alex, my future bride, and a whole slew of fae."

Justice reels back, his slightly less bulky frame filling the doorway. We look a lot alike, only I'm more grizzled and went gray in my teens, and he looks the part of the strapping, dashing prince. "Where do I start?" He runs his hands over his face, a grin taking over.

Tha's another thing Justice does better than me. When I

smile, people recoil. He looks like he was born to be happy, and the territory's been slowly snatching it away from him.

"King Fairbucks had his chance to lock General Klein up, and he failed. My turn. Speaking of failing, Sir Muttrend orchestrated an attack on my carriage. When I dropped off General Klein at the barracks, I sent out an order to have him arrested and taken in." I keep my eyes on the orange in my fist. "I know tha thins out your cabinet, but I can't abide it. My…" I want to tell him I've mated with a lass, but I can't work out the words. So I jump to a safer word, but one tha's just as foreign on my tongue. "My girl-friend was in the carriage, so Mutt's new address is my prison. He'll find a loophole to get himself out soon enough, but for now, tha's where he'll stay. I can't stand to look at his gob another second."

Justice waves his hand like it's all no big deal. "Ye only did me a favor. I've been trying to get him off the cabinet forever, but ye know it has to be a unanimous vote. Cheers, Salem. At least he's off for a little while, until he tugs at tha loophole he always manages to find." A smirk sneaks onto his gob while his eyebrows dance in tha way only a brother can get away with without earning a punch. "Ye finally did it. Ye met someone. Who is she? I'll throw her a grand banquet the moment she comes to meet me." He runs his hand through his hair. "This calls for a celebration. Tonight, even. Tell me, who is she? Who is my new sister?"

I decide not to pull punches, but cut straight to the point, telling the story in the completely wrong order. "She's married to Des, and then she married Alex."

Oh, tha was stupid. Why did I start there?

My brother stills, his lips popping open. "I don't understand. Or maybe now I completely understand why Alexavier isn't here. When did Destino get married and then divorced? Am I really so out of touch? I didn't know a thing about tha. And then Alexavier up and marries Destino's ex?" He shakes his head. "Tha's cold." His nose wrinkles. "But tha's not possible. How could it be? Is she vampire or fae? She can't be both." He picks up two oranges—Lily's oranges—and juggles them while his mouth pulls to the side. "Start over. I missed something."

I don't want to explain the whole thing to my brother, but I know I have to at least try, even though it's not going to make a lick of sense to him. "I'm tired of the fighting between the territories. I know ye are too." Ah, tha's the place to start the story. At the beginning. "I was jumped when I went for a walk in vampire territory a while back. Just walking. We waste a lot of manpower fighting border wars. So Des, Alex and I decided to do something about it. We picked a woman to marry. All three of us wed to the same woman. One woman all the territories would then have to look to."

Justice stumbles backwards, dropping the oranges on the stone floor as if tha'll undo it all. "What? Tha's not a plan!"

I ignore Justice, because it's already done. "So Des married her, and it all blew up in Drexdenberg. Tha's where I was for a long time, making sure they were safe."

Justice casts around for a chair. "I need to sit down.

Maybe I need to lie down. Maybe I need a drink. Maybe ye need a mallet to the head, thinking up stuff like this. King Ronin didn't disinherit Destino for doing this? Like, it actually happened?" He locates a stool at the counter near where I'm squeezing my oranges, his eyes wide as he clutches another he steals from my pile.

"Ronin didn't disinherit Des, though we were worried about tha in the beginning. Ronin's all for the plan. He named Des next in line to receive the crown, actually. Des will sit on the throne in a little less than a year, with his fae wife holding equal power over the vampires."

"What?" Justice blurts, rubbing his temples. "I thought old King Ronin would never give up his rule. Much less to something like this."

"He likes the idea of uniting. Tired of the way things are going, too, I guess. He was happy Des took initiative to fix a problem he couldn't."

It's not meant to be a dig at my brother. We're both doing the best we can. He's not technically king, but all the final decisions fall on his shoulders, ever since our mammy took ill years ago.

I clear my throat. "When King Fairbanks and Queen Kloe balked at Alex marrying the same lass as Des, Ronin stepped in and married them in secret. King Fairbanks *has* to hand the throne down to Alex, so tha's two out of three territories united under her."

"Who is she? Is she a vampire?"

"Fae," I tell him. "Her name is Lily. She's from Neutral Territory, so she doesn't have any real affiliations. Now she's in line to help rule Drexdenberg and Faveda. And before ye ask, she has no magical affinity, so she can't help us get more water."

Justice's expression sours. "Do ye hear yourself? And ye said you're set on marrying her too, aye? Salem, no. This can't work. Ye have no idea what you've done." Then he shakes his head at his words. "But perhaps it's not too late for us. Ye haven't married her yet."

But I know exactly what I've done, and I'd do it all over again, given the opportunity. "My men are tired, Justice. Just because we inherited a disaster doesn't mean we have no responsibility to clean it up. I don't want us all fighting a losing battle until we're old men." I grind the orange harder than I need to. "I already feel like I'm getting old." Lily's young, and I'm... not. Fae and shifter genetics aside, we look strange together. I'm too big, too gray, too dirty. She's slender and lavender and clean, so much tha some-times I'm afraid to touch her.

But I need to.

Justice shakes his head, and for a second, I think he's going to yell at me. But when he speaks, his voice comes out quiet, controlled, and with the authority he uses to rule the throne. "No, Salem. Ye cannot marry this fae woman. I will not allow it."

5

HEADACHE

DESTINO

I watch from the hallway as Justice shakes his head. It's clear Salem's given him too much information to digest. Ever since I left Lily's side to come down here, there's this echo in my mind. A voice I can't decipher that draws my attention. It's Lily's cadence, but I can't understand the individual words. She doesn't sound panicked. I made three half-trips downstairs, bolting back each time I was certain I heard her voice.

Only she promised she hadn't called for me. But though I'm a floor below where she's resting, I can hear her now, her voice in my head. I hear without under-standing, which is quite the predicament. Her tone sounds like she's worried, and also like she's trying to logic herself out of getting worked up. But every time I double back, she gives me her "Of course I'm okay. Why wouldn't I be?"

Now I'm hovering worse than Salem. Splendid.

Salem's gruff voice refocuses me. "Ye can't forbid me from marrying someone, Justice."

"I'm in charge of things while mammy is taking her rest, and I say you're not marrying a fae lass. It's mad, Salem! Do ye even hear yourself?"

"Rule the kingdom all ye like. I'm your brother, not your slave. Ye get full say over the laws of the land, but not who I marry. The only thing ye can control is whether or not you're going to make yourself miserable over it. Have a grand time with tha. It's happening either way, whether ye want a sister or not."

Justice's eyes bug. "A sister? I'll not have it laughed around at pubs tha I've got a fae sister." He hangs his head, and for the life of me, I can't figure out why he grinds the orange in his fist across his forehead. "No, no. And now you're here, which means *she's* here? Tha's the fae lass Vera's so worked up about?"

Salem nods. "Her name is Lily. She's with a healer upstairs. We were attacked on our way in."

"And ye think the territories can unite? Tha anything good can come of our kind intermingling with the fae and vampires? Brother, I know you're an idealist, but I never realized it pushed ye to the point of delusional. There's no way!"

"It's done. The fae and vampires are already going to be under her rule. Uniting with them is wisest, otherwise it's two territories and their pooled resources against just us."

I can't stand back and say nothing anymore. "Think it through," I tell Justice as I enter the kitchen. He angles his chin over his shoulder and growls, no doubt wondering how long I've been listening. "You need more fertile land and water, and the fae can't grow the plumapples on their soil that could heal a lot of their maladies. Think of how beautiful Jacoba could be if you shared resources—if the fae helped you build your territory. If you were united."

"Did ye leave Lily alone with the healer?" Salem shouts at me.

I wince at his volume when it adds to Lily's indecipherable cadence that's still playing in my head. "Settle, brother. Healer Wesley gave her something for the pain after she was stitched up, and I walked him out the front door. She's not with anyone up there. She's lying down to take a nap."

To his credit, Justice sticks a wary hand in my direction. "I hear congratulations are in order. Ye got yourself one-third of a wife."

My smile is stiff at the implication that Lily isn't wholly mine. "The future queen of Drexdenberg and Faveda is resting upstairs, and shouldn't be disturbed. We can spend a bit more time talking about unification, yeah?" Though I can still hear Lily's cadence, poking at my brain and challenging me to get to the bottom of this puzzle I cannot understand. I plop down on a stool and smack Justice on the meat of his bicep. "Just three blokes mucking about, planning out better days ahead."

Justice is dubious at best. "What makes ye think I need the help of a fae? They're not good for anything but looking superior."

"Ah, but you're wrong. Faveda is lush and beautiful."

"Beauty only matters to the vain."

"Beauty matters to the beasts as well. I know your wells are drying up. I know it's getting harder for you to graze. An alliance could solve all of your problems, though it would require you to think of the good of your people, valuing their wellbeing over your prejudices and pride. Tough decision, that."

Justice shoots Salem a scathing look for spilling Jacoba's weaknesses to me, but Salem is unapologetic. "We won't last much longer if we don't take the help tha's right across our borders. I know ye care about the people more than ye worship your pride. So I'm going to marry Lily. Tha way we'll all be united."

Justice shakes his head. "But she'll never be queen of Jacoba. *I* would have to marry her for tha to happen, and I'm not as sold on this mad plan as ye are."

Everything in Salem tightens at the notion of his brother marrying Lily. I lift my palm in Salem's direction, trying to communicate tranquility. "Settle, Salem." Lily's voice in my head is still muddling my thoughts, though I can't understand her. I wonder if I'm more exhausted than I realized. Still, I can't leave to go back to her now. If I don't keep Salem calm while he gets used to his mate bond, he might attack his own brother, which is a thing for which he'd never forgive himself.

Salem pitches the orange rinds into the compost bin with more force than necessary. "Ye won't marry her. *I* will. She might not be queen of Jacoba, but she'll have partial control over our militia because she'll rule by my side. Tha's good enough."

Justice hangs his head. "I suppose there's no talking ye out of this?"

"It's done," I tell him, rubbing my temples. Lily's voice is louder the further away from her I get. When I get off my stool and step toward the hallway but still remain in the kitchen, the volume softens just enough to let me think. "Lily's my wife, and Alex's. If she agrees, she'll be Salem's wife, too." I move back into the kitchen and slap Justice on the back, hoping he rallies. "The world is changing, yeah? Best not fall behind the curve on this one. They need their leaders to lead, not constantly react to the latest fire that needs snuffing out."

"Easy for ye to say when it's not ye they scream at when their world burns."

"It will be," I remind him, noting the bags under his eyes. "And when my time comes, I don't want the same problems the kings and queens before me couldn't solve. I want something better for my people. Deep down, I know you do, too. You're a brilliant ruler, Justice. Always have been. Sometimes the road to a better life doesn't look like we think it should. But it's there, if you can learn to look for it."

My temples feel hot through the beginnings of a headache. Lily's voice is too loud where I'm standing, so I move to stand in the doorway.

"It's dangerous, what you're doing. Ye may have goodness in your heart and grand plans on your mind, but the people are going to revolt. They'll hate her for forcing them into a change none of them asked to be part of. You've painted a target on her back. If I wasn't so angry at ye all for pulling this stunt behind my back, I'd actually feel sorry for all you're putting her through. Fae are delicate, and you're thrusting her in front of the bullseye."

Salem strains the orange juice, because he's that sensitive to Lily's tastes. "We look out for each other."

"Aye." Then Justice stands, his shoulders rolling back as he tosses the orange from one fist to the other. "All the same, I'd like to have a chat with the lass. She's going to be my sister, after all. Politics aside, I want to hear her take on it." Justice sighs heavily. "Of all the things I want for ye, Salem, a strategic marriage isn't on the list."

Salem's jaw is firm. "Of all the things I want for my people, dying because we're too stubborn to ask for water isn't on the list. Lily is Alex's wife; he won't let her die. If she's here, he'll send people to make sure she and her people have water."

"But we are not her people!" Justice argues. "I wanted more for ye than this!"

Every now and then when I listen to Justice openly care about Salem's wellbeing, I wish Alex and Salem were my actual brothers. The fact that we're united with Lily brings that dream closer to reality. It's nice to see the two care about each other, that Salem has someone when Alex and I aren't around.

"Des, grab the tray over there, will ye?" Salem asks, ignoring his brother. Justice isn't a bad guy. In fact, he's a decent bloke. It's Salem who's never learned to fully let him in. Alex and I have to fight tooth and nail for Salem to let us near the smallest bit of his heart when it's bleeding.

When I move toward the stack of trays in the far corner of the kitchen, I realize I've taken about four steps too many from Lily's bedroom. Her volume is full-shout, though her words are still indecipherable. My head feels like it's trapped in a vice, tightening too much ever since I left her side. I need to lie down. I don't understand what my deal is, and why my head hurts the further I get from Lily.

I take eight more steps toward the stack of trays on the opposite end of the kitchen, but stop, not even halfway there. "I don't think I can," I admit, pointing to my head. Lily's voice is so loud now, I know I must be shouting. I want to be helpful, but I can't go a step farther, or I'm afraid I might go deaf from her voice ramping up in my head. "It's too loud!"

Salem is saying something, but I can't hear him.

I can't hear anything but Lily's deafening cadence thrumming through my body.

6

THE PRICE OF SEPARATING

DESTINO

I take another half a step toward the trays and fall to my knees, covering my ears as if that'll do anything. "Make it stop!" I cry, my eyes watering from the pressure of her voice. My nose is suddenly wet, but I can't move my hands from my ears to swipe at it. I need a caffure pill. A hammer to the head. Something to make the pain stop.

Salem's kneeling by my side in the next breath, and Justice crouches in front of me. They're saying things, but I can't hear them. They look scared, and I know I'm the one frightening them. Justice reaches into his pocket and pulls out a handkerchief, dabbing at my nose and pulling it away to show me that I'm bleeding. I have a bloody nose. Out of nowhere.

"Lily's shouting!" I tell them, half-explaining my conundrum.

Salem's on his feet and bolting for the stairs, though that's not actually going to solve the problem. "Get me to the hallway!" I beg Salem's brother. That seems to be the only thing that quieted the shouting.

Justice holds the handkerchief to my nose and helps me to my feet. I stumble along beside him, my headache lessening with every step I take towards Lily. I can breathe without pain now. I can open my eyes without wincing. Her voice is still there, but it's not excruciating to hear. Just a dull roar, like waves crashing in the background of my mind.

Justice leans me against the wall. "Is it better? Ye looked like ye might have a stroke or something."

My breath comes out in hard pants. "Better now. Cheers, Justice. I need to get to Lily."

"What is it with this lass tha's got Salem and ye all twisted up? I don't understand."

I don't have it in me to explain that what started out as a chess move is now something I can't shake. I take Lily with me everywhere I go, and now when we're apart, it feels wrong. It physically hurts me to be separated from her. I stumble up the steps, and the closer I get, the better I feel. I can't hear her murmured shouting in my mind at all as I round the corner and trip over my own feet, catching myself on the wall. My headache lifts, like a veil I've no need for as I bolt toward Salem's bedroom.

I bang open the door to find Salem examining her stitches with a skeptical eye. They both jump at my entrance, but my headache is finally gone, so I don't care that I've startled them. "You were shouting," I explain.

"I just went over this with Salem. I didn't say a single word. Oh, your nose! What happened? Are you okay?"

"Are *you* okay?" I ask her, tucking my shirt back in and straightening so I don't look as disheveled as I feel.

"Dog bite aside, I'm fine. You two have really ramped up the intensity lately, huh. Is there something wrong that I don't know about? Some reason I should be on edge?"

I shake my head. "No more than usual. Something's wrong, though. The further away from you I get, I can hear what sounds like your voice in my head. The more we're separated, the louder it gets, until it feels like my brain is splitting in half."

"Are you serious? The distance—your headache—gave you a nosebleed? That's not psychosomatic."

I nod, grateful the motion doesn't cause me a lick of pain. "I don't understand any of it, only that the price of separating isn't one I'll be willing to pay again any time soon. I do hope you don't grow tired of the sight of me."

"You're hearing me when I'm not even speaking? What am I saying?"

"I can't make out a single word, but I know it's you."

"How?"

"Because I know your voice." I don't mean for that to come out sappy and romantic, but that's precisely how it hangs in the air between us. I see her swoon, and I feel something similar echo in my own chest. I *do* know her voice. "I look forward to you," I admit. Yeah, that's disgustingly sappy. But it's true, and she's the kind of woman who deserves to hear true things.

Her neck shrinks, and it's just about the cutest thing I've ever seen. "I look forward to you, too."

Justice stalks into the room with his chest puffed, taking in the sight of Lily leaning against Salem's headboard, gaunt and sleepy. "I look forward to speaking with ye. Lily, is it? I'm Prince Justice, Salem's older brother."

Justice is huge, almost as big as Salem. Though Salem's always been the surlier one to look at, the one everyone's fearful of, Lily shrinks in Justice's presence. "Pleased to meet you, your majesty." She makes to get out of bed, but Salem holds his hands up. "Salem, I'm supposed to bow. He's royalty."

Salem's jaw is set. "Not a single toe is going to touch on this floor, aye? Ye were attacked. Justice doesn't need the bowing."

Justice tucks his hands behind to rest on the small of his back, trying to look proper, as he always does when he's addressing the territory. "I hear you're the one bringing controversy and change into my land. I can wait until you've rested and eaten before we discuss your scheme, but not much longer than tha. I'll see ye after supper tonight in the throne room to discuss *your* plans for *my* people."

Lily nods. "Yes, your majesty."

"Enough, Justice," Salem chides with a growl.

Justice points at the ground in a stabby motion. "No,

Salem. If this lass is part of your plan, I need to know what she's up to. I deserve to know who's living under my roof."

Justice doesn't argue any more than that, but turns on his heel and shuts the door behind him, leaving us to trade anxious glances while silence falls around us.

7

DINING WITH THE BOYS

LILYA

I've never been clumsier in my entire life. Eating at the wood-hewn table with Justice, Salem and Des sets my teeth on edge. I'm ravenous, but knowing that I'm going to have to sit down and chat with Justice after the meal has my stomach churning with dread. They eat lots of root vegetables here, so the parsnip mash is accompanied by a thick brown gravy that's also ladled over the grainy bread, which is rougher to chew than steak.

It's cute to watch Salem in his home, his elbows on the table and ankle looped around mine where no one can see. While the other tables in the vampire and fae royal families were long and regal, this one is simpler. Honest. Built just big enough for a family of four. Maybe it's the normal dining room, and they use a different one for big, fancy occasions. Or maybe they don't care about big, fancy occasions. The wooden table warms the stone-walled room, adding a touch of togetherness in the cold mansion. I like these close quarters, that my feet can touch both Des and Salem, and I'm not too far from Justice that I can't read the shadows in his slate eyes whenever he looks at me.

He's calculating something. Still sizing me up to see if I can be trusted. I'm not sure what test I'm supposed to be passing while I eat, but I haven't aced it yet, because Justice is still casting me skeptical glances every time I shovel some of the mash into my mouth.

"The troops were fine without ye," Justice tells Salem. "Ye trained your captains well."

"Tha's good to know. We're not at war, so I didn't see the harm in stepping away for a few. Part of the border wall fell, so when I dropped off my prisoner on the way in, I sent a battalion to clear away the debris. But I'm not having them reconstruct it."

He leaves the decision with no room for discussion, putting his foot down that unity is on the horizon. There's no use rebuilding a wall if he intends to have it torn down.

I'm so proud of this great man. It shocks me every time someone so incredible looks at me like I might be worth his time.

Justice skates over the possible tension. "Ye should take a break more often. Some time off looks good on ye, brother."

I watch for signs of Salem being played, for his time away to mean that another agenda had room to push its way in, but I don't get that vibe from Justice. He looks genuinely glad for his brother getting a break.

"Tha's why we want this merger," Salem replies,

segueing into our agenda. "If we aren't fighting each other over boundary lines and trade agreements, our people can work on unconditioning themselves to be ready for war. Befriend the enemy, and there isn't one to fight anymore. War is exhausting us all."

"Is tha what you're doing with Destino and Lily, here? Befriending the enemy?"

Salem stiffens, though I can tell by the honesty beaming from Justice's lowered shoulders that he didn't mean anything bad by it. Salem leans forward, jabbing his fork in Justice's direction. "Watch it, Brother. Ye know Des has been my best mate since we were tikes. And I'm not befriending Lily. I'm in love with her. Get a good look at your future sister-in-law, because I'll be marrying her as soon as she gets settled."

It's the second time he's mentioned marrying me, and both times, I don't know what to do with it. Did I miss the part where he asked for my hand? Is it just assumed that we're getting married? I don't know why this hits me in both the right and the wrong ways, but my nose scrunches in time with my heart swelling and cresting.

"What?" Salem asks of my grimace.

I don't want to talk about this in front of Justice. "It's nothing."

Salem looks close to vomiting out of nowhere. "Whenever ye brush anything off, I know it's big. What?"

I draw a line through my root vegetable mash, keeping my eyes from all three of them. "You've said something like that before, that you're going to marry me, but you've never actually asked me. It's backwards. Like you're deciding for me rather than bringing me into the process."

Salem rears back, his face horror-stricken as the color drains from it. "Ye don't want to marry me?"

I make an X through my mash. "I didn't say that. Forget it. I shouldn't have said anything. Now it's a whole big thing. It just would've been nice to be asked, is all."

Des rests his head in his hands, as if he's tired of dealing with buffoons. "You didn't ask her, mate? I thought you must've, given how you talk about it as if it's a done deal."

I don't want to dig my heels in on this, and I know I've gone along fine with everything so far. But I'd at least like to be presented with the choice, rather than go along with it all as if I have no ownership in the plan. It's not the three of them plus their token uterus. It's the four of us.

My voice is small when it finally comes, but it's there. "I kind of want to know that even if uniting the territories wasn't on the radar, that you'd still choose me. That I'd be the one. For Des and Alex, it was an arrangement that love blossomed from afterwards. I don't want it to be like that with us."

Salem looks as if I've just told him he's fat. He picks up his chair and moves it so it's touching mine, and then plops back down so there's not an inch of space between us for confusion to fester. "Ye don't know tha I love ye? Tha you're the only one I've ever had eyes for? After all we've been through, ye don't know ye own my heart?"

I hate that we're having this conversation in front of his brother, so I hide. My face buries itself in the meat of his shoulder, letting me inhale the masculine scent of him that's always drawn me in. He smells like freshly-cut pine and something spicy I can't believe I ever lived without.

Though he's clearly confused, his fingers find their way to the back of my head, burying themselves in my curls. I love when he sticks his nose on the top of my head and inhales deeply. It feels like I belong, not like I have to do my best to fit in. It's like all the things I'm not and all the wretched things I am don't have to make excuses for themselves. He's strong enough to hold all the facets of me, and gentle enough not to break them or fix them out of turn.

"I know you love me," I tell him. "I just need to know that this is your choice, not your obligation. It's easier to duck out of an obligation than it is your choice."

Maybe I was always Lexi's obligation.

No, not Lexi. Prince Alexavier.

I try not to think about Alexavier; the whole thing is too painful to look at directly just yet.

"I choose ye," Salem promises in a whisper. "I will make sure ye never walk alone."

It's the most beautiful thing he could say, and he does so without qualification. He doesn't cast his brother an embarrassed look at being so emotionally vulnerable; he owns it, even as we go back to eating with me swallowed up in his burly side.

Justice gapes at his brother as if Salem's grown a third eyeball.

"How's your headache?" I ask Des when Salem engages

Justice in asking for updates about the territory that happened while he was away.

Des' smile isn't pained anymore, so I know he's telling me the truth when he answers, "Completely gone. Seems like you're the golden cure for what ails me." His grin falters. "I don't understand it, though. Why does it feel like my head is going to explode when I'm farther away from you? I had a bloody nose, so I know it's not just mental."

It's no small worry to me, this new development we've tested a few times this afternoon. Every time Des gets down the stairs and through a few hallways while I'm in the bedroom, his headache starts to come back. "I guess we'll just have to stick close for a while. There are worse problems, right?"

My hand finds his under the table, our littlest fingers hooking together. We both calm at the simple touch, and I wonder if I'm centering him, or if he's soothing me.

He drops my finger but moves his seat closer to mine, because we want to be close, but he still needs his left hand to eat, since his right arm is still immobile. We finish the meal like that, with the guys hemming me in, and I wouldn't have it any other way.

When I move to stand, Justice finally addresses me directly—a thing we've managed to avoid throughout the entire meal. "You'll stay here, Lily. I need a word. Several, in fact."

My stomach flips. "Alright."

Salem and Des sit back down, but Justice shakes his head. "Out ye go, lads. I'll return her in one piece."

Though Justice is the standing ruler of Jacoba, both the guys pause for my nod before leaving the dining room.

Justice waits until we're alone before he cuts to the chase. "Ye seem like a sweet lass, so I'll not dance around it. My brother is only marrying ye because our land needs water. If you're tied to Alexavier, the fae people won't permit their princess to die in a land tha could be easily fixed by a few more wells. But do not trick yourself into believing it's more than tha." Justice's words steal the breath from my lungs, but when he levels his gaze at me, I know the worst is yet to come. He doesn't look cruel but emotionless when he says, "Salem belongs to another lass."

8

INTERROGATION BY JUSTICE

LILYA

I refuse to get emotional in front of this stranger, but the urge to run away from this conversation is strong. Still, I make a silent promise that I will force myself to belong anywhere Salem resides. Even if I'm the only fae for miles, I will make this my home because Salem loves this place. He fights to protect it. "You're lying. The guys would've told me if Salem had a girlfriend."

Justice dips his chin. "Maybe Destino and Alexavier don't know. Salem is a private lad. But I assure ye, there are things brothers only confess to each other, and yet other things Salem won't tell even me. I've overheard him telling our mammy tha he's in love when he goes to sit by her bedside. Sneaks out to visit the lass every so often. Says he's 'going to check the north border' but he heads in the opposite direction every time. Comes back a couple days later with a secretive look to him and wee smiles he tries to hide. But I see them. I always see him."

I bite down on my lower lip. "I don't believe you. Salem doesn't lie to me, and I'm not the type to steal another girl's boyfriend. If you want me gone, we can talk about that without you going and making things up."

Maybe that's too bold, but I'm tired, my leg is sore, and I don't want to deal with this right now. Or ever. Lexi ditching out is one thing.

Alexavier, not Lexi. Prince Alexavier.

To think of Salem leaving, too? I shake my head at myself. I know I'm being selfish, loving the three of them and expecting fidelity in return. But that was the agreement. That's what we all wanted.

Justice leans back in his seat across the table from me and folds his thick arms over his chest. He's built like Salem, which is to say he's intimidating even when he's not trying to be. Sizing me up as he is, I'm acutely aware of how small I am.

"I do want ye gone," he admits, and my palms start to sweat. "Or, I did, anyway. I don't understand it all. There are parts of your plan tha are barking mad, but Salem's right tha we can't keep things going as they are. Our wells are drying up. An alliance with the fae isn't ideal, but it makes sense. But the vampires? I fail to see how tha's necessary. They've done more harm to us than the fae. The fae just ignore us while we're struggling. The vampires get aggressive. They draw blood. I can't imagine how ye want me to pitch an alliance with them to Jacoba."

I run my tongue over my top row of teeth while I think through his words and pick out the ones I can deal with. "I appreciate that you're being direct. We don't have to like each other. I'd rather know what I'm dealing with than have you smile at me while plotting to stab me in my sleep."

His eyebrows lift into his hairline. He looks so much like Salem, but with subtle differences. His hair isn't gray. He's clean-shaven. His shoulders perhaps aren't as broad as Salem's. But everything else is so very similar. Justice's chin tilts to the side as his eyes narrow. "Is tha what ye think of shifters? Tha we're a bunch of violent lowlifes?"

I band my arms over my stomach, holding myself while I try to keep my chin level and appear as if I have some semblance of bravery in my arsenal. "You forget I was raised in Neutral Territory. I know that enemies come in all forms. I've had my life endangered by shifters, by vampires and by the fae. I'm not naïve enough to think one race turned out more horrible than the others. It's all different shades of the same bad color." I lean forward, hoping I make sense to Justice, that I'm not the skinny idiot this all happens around, but that I help craft the change on purpose. "All we're trying to do is make people see that we're not so different. The things that make us the same far outnumber the things that divide us. We all need better resources. We all need kindness and a neighbor who cares if we die alone. We need to respect and trust the people in authority so everyone doesn't feel the weight of the world on their shoulders when they struggle to find their optimism. And frankly, optimism shouldn't be in such short supply."

Justice blinks three times, clearly unprepared for me to have an actual response. "I assumed this was one of Alexavier's hairbrained schemes he managed to talk Destino and Salem into, but perhaps it was your idea."

I let out an airy laugh through my nose. "Your first guess was right. It was Prince Alexavier's idea. It was a good one. The three of us agreed this was what the world needed to move forward. Aren't you tired?" I lean back, hoping I don't look confrontational. "Aren't you bored of the same battles over and over? Don't you want help for your territory?"

"Help tha comes at the expense of power is no help to me."

"What power do you imagine anyone would be taking from you? It'll still be three territories, but this time without borders. Your family will still rule over Jacoba. They'll need you more than ever. You'll still maintain control and make the laws for your people. But you can't keep the world out if you want your people to thrive. That's not how life works."

Justice laces his fingers together behind his head, digesting my words as he leans back in his chair that he's rocking on its back two legs. "Okay, let's say you're right and I agree. The second we take those borders down, it's going to be chaos. My people hate the vampires. All tha resentment isn't going to go away in a blink."

"I guess we'll need your help, then. Perhaps you'll still play a crucial role in setting the tone for how the world is going to be, instead of putting up with how it's always been."

Justice isn't satisfied. I can tell by his irritable huff. "Tha's going to take years. I mean right now. What's the plan for lowering the aggression before we lower the walls?"

This is good. He's considering the idea enough to help form a plan. It's not everything, but it's a very big something. "You know your people better than I do. Any ideas?"

"But ye lived in Neutral Territory, where the races *have* to get along, more or less. How does tha work?"

My mouth pulls to the side as I think. I pick up my fork and drum a slow staccato rhythm on the table. "We don't have a choice, and we're all coming off the tail end of pretty awful situations. Everyone in Neutral Territory understands that their neighbor just had the crap beat out of them by life. It works because we don't have ties to our own people anymore." I let out a long sigh. "I'm not sure I'm being all that helpful."

"Not really, but tha's good to know. I didn't realize there were any fae in Neutral Territory."

I stare at my fork as it taps. "There aren't, now that I don't live there. The fae don't believe in a punishment like that. Not as easy to slowly pick at someone if they're banished."

"Then how'd ye end up there?"

I squirm in my seat. "Neutral Territory was a lot safer for me than Faveda. General Klein isn't the fatherly type. Bad luck for him he ended up with a daughter like me, I guess." I don't like the bitter note in my tone. It makes it seem like I feel bad about the whole situation, which isn't something I want to carry around on my sleeve.

Justice lets out a low whistle. "You're General Klein's daughter? He's a right bastard. I didn't know he had a daughter."

"Well, after trying to kill me again, all he's going to have is a jail cell, thanks to your brother being amazing." I grip the nape of my neck and rub, wishing we were talking about anything but that. "It's nice in Neutral Territory. They don't have the need to hide who they are. The crimes are all laid bare on the table, so there's less pretending. It's easier, in a way."

"Ah. Well, tha's much different than Faveda. Swindlers, the whole lot of them."

I shrug, unwilling to play this game. "I think that's the place we start—ironing out any hate speech from our rulers. Maybe sit down with Ronin, Des, Salem, King Fairbanks and Prince Alexavier." I don't know how to ask my next question, so I just go for it. "Your mother isn't... She isn't ruling anymore?"

A muscle in Justice's jaw ticks. "No. She's not able. Would ye like to meet her?"

"Really?" My spine straightens against the hard back of my seat.

"Aye. I reckon it'll be harder for ye to tell a lie to a dying woman. But you're fae, so I wouldn't put it past ye."

I stand abruptly, my shoulders rolling back. "I'm no

more fae than you are. If I was a shifter coming to you with this plan, would you have this big a problem with it?"

Justice stands, making my height laughable as he comes around the side of the table to tower over me. "Probably not. But ye are what ye are. No getting around tha."

When he walks out of the room after insulting me to my face, I follow until I hear Des' howl of pain. "Ah! Lily, where are you?"

I spin around and bolt in the direction of Des' voice, throwing my arms around him the second he comes into view from upstairs. "I'm sorry! I forgot about the tether. Are you okay?"

Des squinches his eyes tight and nods, though his heart is racing against mine. "I think so. Felt like a nail was drilling through my temple. I'll go with you. Wherever it is, we'll go together."

I nod, my cheek pressing into the side of his neck. "Of course."

Justice grumbles his discontent at the sight of our connection. "Let's go, then."

I link my littlest finger through Des'. Though he doesn't know where I'm headed, he walks beside me anyway.

9

MOTHER BUTCHER

LILYA

$\mathscr{N}$ine. Mother Butcher

Lilya

IT'S NOT the best impression I'd like to give when I meet Salem's mother for the first time, but given that she's got her eyes closed and there's no guarantee she can hear me, I guess things could be worse. Mrs. Butcher has gray hair, just like Salem, but hers looks earned by time, since she appears to be in her late sixties. Her hands rest motionless at her sides while her chest moves in a shallow rhythm. She's dressed in a black velvet gown that's every bit regal as it is a statement: this is a room for mourning, though Queen Butcher isn't altogether passed yet.

The room is small but nice, with the standard stone walls and floors decorated with light blue tapestries and a rug lined with gold thread—simplicity married with a touch of something lovely. Incense is burning in the corner, filling the room with a sandalwood stench so thick, it's hard to pick out notes of anything else.

Queen Butcher is laid out on a bed near the window, the sun highlighting the wrinkles around her mouth and eyes. I wonder what her plans were for her kingdom, and how she would feel about the changes that are about to take place on her soil.

I wonder if she would've liked me. If she could've gotten past the fact that I'm fae and seen how much I truly love her son, and want a brighter future for her people.

"Should I ask Salem before I talk to his mom?" I ask Des, twisting the edge of my t-shirt between my fingers as I stand in the doorway. I'm afraid to go in any further, worried I'm intruding on something sacred.

Des shrugs. "I'm sure it's fine. What's he going to say? Marry me but don't meet my mum? Besides, Salem went out for a bit."

Out. How perfectly nondescript. Maybe Des knows about Salem's girlfriend, which is where he probably slipped off to.

Des rubs his five o'clock shadow with his left hand. "Said he was going to go check on the north border."

Justice catches my eye, giving me a smug look that's perfectly timed with my heart sinking.

I feel foolish, and like our team is splintering further

with all the half-truths roaming about in the air. But I'm the fae, so of course it's me who's suspect for every little fib.

If Salem needs the space to see his girlfriend, I have to give him that. I can apologize to her later, make her see that I didn't know he was taken. Our master plan aside, I just can't do that to another woman, even though I'm crazy for him.

Justice follows us when we step inside, though I wish he would stop hovering. It's like he wants to watch every move I make, while wanting to be nowhere near me. "Can I have a minute alone with her?" I ask the guys.

"No," Justice rules, his mouth firm. He's got his hands tucked behind his back, which makes him look regal and brimming with deep thoughts.

"You think I'm going to hurt her?" I ask, affronted. "Then why show me where she's at? I could sneak in here any time and off her, if that's what I wanted. Think it through, man."

Justice frowns at me as the truth in my words rings in his ears. "Fine. But I'll need to pat ye down before you're alone with my mammy."

I hold my arms out to the sides, scowling at him as he does a professional job of feeling under my arms, down my legs and the small of my back and stomach. My dagger and holster are upstairs. "Satisfied?"

Justice points to the door. "I'll be right out here, so don't think of pulling any fae-like trickery."

I fight the urge to stick out my tongue at him, and wait

for Des and Justice to leave the room. When I hear the door click, I exhale. "That's better." I limp closer, though I'm careful not to touch her or the bed. I clear my throat three times, worried I'll say the wrong thing. Though, it's not like she's going to be verbal about my mistakes, so when I open my mouth, I go for the bare truth. "I'm in love with your son."

It feels strangely liberating to fill the air with those words. Though I don't know much about the woman, I hope she's the sort who feels happy knowing her child is loved.

"I'm on the fence about Justice, though. He's not a bad guy, but he's a bit of a judgmental prick. He cares about your people, which I guess is what counts." I twist the hem of my shirt between two fingers. "I'm probably not who you imagined your son ending up with, so how about I promise you I'll be respectful of your culture. I'll be kind and stick by his side even when the world doesn't understand us. I'm not sure if that'll make you happy or angry, but either way, I think you did a great job raising him. He's..." I rub my sweaty palms off on my jeans. "Salem doesn't waste words, like I do. Like everyone does. He doesn't waste his punches, either. He says the right thing and fights only for what he believes in. Jacoba is lucky to have him leading their army." My mind drifts to the stack of napkins in his breast pocket. "He's romantic, and more sensitive than people give him credit for. If I ever had a son, I'd want him to have those qualities."

Then it dawns on me like a boulder thrown at my head

that I will never have any children. Fae can't reproduce outside their species. It's not possible. Prince Alexavier is my husband in name only, which means I will never have a child. I reach out to brace myself on the stone wall, the chill reaching through my arm and crawling through the rest of me.

It's silly to be this gut-punched over something I never thought to want. Meeting a man of my species wasn't even a possibility until a couple months ago. The thought of having kids of my own isn't something I ever entertained with any real conviction. I mean, the thought did cross my mind when Prince Alexavier and I married, but we never talked about it. That was far too soon.

And now it's never.

"I can't give you any grandchildren," I confess, frustrated with myself that my tone comes across mournful over something I shouldn't care this much about. I pry my hand from the wall and force myself to stand, to stomach this truth because that's what it is. There is no getting around it. "You probably want some cute little crawlers, but I can't give them to you. I'm fae, and Salem isn't. I have a fae husband, but we're..." It's hard to say the words. "We've separated, so that's that." A nervous laugh bubbles out of me, and I wonder if I've tipped the edge into partial insanity. "I never knew my birth mother, so it's probably just as well. I don't know the first thing about children. I haven't been around any since I was one, and that didn't end so well." I'm shaking my head. Why can't I stop shaking my head? "It's good. This is good. One less thing to worry about." I hate the pathetic false cheer in my voice, and I'm grateful she can't really hear me, can't see my lower lip tremble through my brave attempt at a smile.

Why am I upset about this? It's nothing I was super passionate about before. It's the finality of the verdict I'm having a hard time choking down.

I clear my throat again and change the subject, giving her updates on uniting the territories, and why it's so important to me. "Salem was jumped in vampire territory for just going on a walk."

And these hideous scars down my face are from a shifter attacking a little girl.

Of course, I don't mention that, but I feel the sting afresh, and check over my shoulder to make sure the bear who left me alive hasn't sneaked back in to finish the job.

I'm being ridiculous.

"They didn't realize he was royalty, of course, but still, it's a dark world if people can't go strolling down certain streets. He's brave for wanting more for his people, for putting himself out there like that. I think you would be proud of him fighting for what he believes in by using strategy and political moves rather than knives. I think he's incredible. All three of the princes are. They concocted this thing together."

I ramble on, my words a mix of admiration for her son and apologies for everything I am that she probably wouldn't approve of.

It's oddly satisfying to unburden myself of my ambitions to another woman. I miss Fiora terribly, but I don't let myself dwell on that. Our time isn't over.

A terrible thought strikes me across the chest. Is my time with my mother over? Fiora can't come to Jacoba. She was banned for… reasons. Reasons she never saw fit to tell me.

"I miss my mom," I confess to Mother Butcher. "Maybe I'm too old for that, but I can't help it. She would know what to do, who to be. I don't have any clue how to do this, how to be good for your people, for your son." I touch the footboard, unsure if that's considered disrespectful. "If it's alright with you, I want to pretend that you're my mom. That you want me in your family. That you have buckets of gentleness stored up just for me. This… This is hard."

Of course, she doesn't answer.

Before I hit the hallway, tears threaten my composure, but this is not the time. Honestly, I highly doubt it'll ever be the time to break down. There's a long road ahead of us, and I worry there will be nothing left of me if I dissolve into a puddle right now. But the ache in my chest grows when I think of the very real rule that my mother will never see me in the shifter mansion. She will never come to dinner here and see me in her homeland.

I wonder if I'm powerless to bring my family to me. If that's true, I pray I can content myself with the family I've created, broken as we are.

10

A LILY IN NATURE

DESTINO

I can't bring myself to speak, even as Lily falls into my arms. Correction, my arm. I can only hold her with my left, my right wrist dangling useless at my side.

I want to reassure her, but her upset is something I can't fix. I can't give her a child. The only one of us who can is Alex, who's too stupid to understand the amazing gift life handed to us.

She doesn't get misty-eyed over it. She pretends nothing at all is wrong as I hold her in the hallway, rocking us slowly from side to side. I shake my head slightly at Justice, making sure he knows we're to let her keep her secrets she left between herself and his mum. She doesn't know we heard every word, so I let her have her illusion of privacy.

But it kills me that she desires something I can't give her. Something I didn't think to ask her if she wanted. It's a hard pill to swallow, this ramification of our decisions. I never thought much about having children, but now that possibility is gone from me, too. My bloodline will come to an end, and I'll need to find a way to make my peace with that.

Justice opens his mouth, but I bare my fangs at him to shut him up. He's not afraid of me, as most shifters are of vampires. He knows I would never bite him, using my teeth as weapons. But the message is delivered clear enough: Lily doesn't need our commentary on her life. He got front row seats to her tender insides without invitation.

I love the way Lily fits in my arm, her face tucked in the crook of my neck as if we were carved from the same piece of granite and sliced apart by life and time. She belongs right here. I thumb the small bandage on her neck that covers over my bite mark. I probably shouldn't feel some baser pride that she let me mark her. It's brutish to indulge in fantasies of us doing that again. Though, as there isn't blood here for me, I'm fairly certain it won't be more than a day or so before I'm thirsty again. "Let's go for a walk around the mansion, yeah? There's a nice garden out back you'll like. The sun's about to set, but we can bring a lantern."

"That sounds nice. We won't be attacked?"

She asks me the question, but her eyes flick to Justice, who gives her a solemn half-bow. "I'll speak to the guards to make sure you're left untouched. Take your time, Miss Lily."

"Your majesty," I correct him, even though he's finally making a show of being respectful. "She's a princess twice over. That's more clout than either of us have."

Justice's jaw tightens, but he doesn't speak his displeasure. "Your majesty."

I keep my arm around her back and hold her hand while we walk, as if her body is as fragile as Fiora's, and needs me to shelter her from the storm we've created. We leave Justice behind, moving into the early twilight the second I'm able. It's a splendid time for me, because I can see well enough to enjoy the world without lanterns, while walking around in plain sight without fearing the sun.

The whole of Jacoba used to be far greener, but in the past few years, the land has grown brown and parched. There are rows of homes, whole neighborhoods and cities in the distance that are bustling with life, but it's quiet on the mansion grounds, the air whistling too harshly since there are hardly any leaves on the trees to remind it to slow down.

I take Lily to the herb garden first, knowing fae are drawn to nature. "When Alex is feeling lost, he either finds his way to something green, or he makes his world greener by forcing nature's hand." I kiss her temple because I can't not. "Alex actually grew this bit for Salem. He tends it every now and then. The ground here isn't fertile enough on its own for fragile things like herbs."

Her hands are tremulous as she kneels awkwardly in the grass, babying her injured leg, as Healer Wesley instructed. She brushes her fingers over the delicate tips of the basil leaves. "Neutral Territory is black and grey. Everything is rocky and dirty. There's barely any nature the further in you get. A few trees, but nothing like Faveda." She smells the leaf but doesn't smile. Her eyes are aimed at the plant, but her gaze seems very far away, as if she's gone somewhere entirely other in her mind.

"That must've been difficult for you."

"Hmm." Lily bows her head and rocks twice, her angst growing. Then just as quickly as it rises, she fends it off by going motionless. It's like she's afraid to feel anything, because then she might feel too much—more than she's ready for just yet. I can't say I blame her, but it's a sad sight to see from this angle. I long to hold her, but I wager she wouldn't want that right now. Just being near feels like the right move—there to grab onto if she needs me.

When she finally speaks, she's so quiet, I have to lean in to listen. "I don't think the fae are weak for not sending their people to Neutral Territory. I think they're strategic in keeping the green for themselves. Part of the punishment of living in Neutral Territory is that not even nature wants to exist in a place like that. If a fae was knowingly exiled there, they would make Neutral Territory beautiful, which would lessen the punishment of the criminals there." I kneel beside her, watching her throat constrict as her nerves spike. "It was painful, being separated from nature for most of my life. I was constantly cold on the inside, like I didn't belong anywhere."

I band my arm around her back and rub her bicep. "You belong here with me, yeah?" Her skin is chilly. Why does she never complain about these things? I need to get better at anticipating the needs she'll never voice. I don't have a jacket to offer her. What a shoddy husband I'm turning out to be.

"Salem has a girlfriend," she blurts out, her eyes fixated on the basil leaves as if they've betrayed her. "Why didn't you tell me?"

I can't help my frown. "Other than you? No, he doesn't."

"He does. Justice told me he's been in love with this other woman for years. It explains why he never made a move. Why he set me up with you and Prince Alexavier. I feel so stupid. I would never do that to another woman."

She's calling Alex by his full name and title now? I guess that's not unexpected, but it's significant to me. Lily's in serious pain, no matter how quiet she tries to keep it. And now this mystery fictional girlfriend of Salem's? I pull her closer, my arms around her to shoulder at least a portion of all that's weighing her down. "Blue eyes, it's not true. Maybe there are things Salem tells Justice that he doesn't tell Alex and me, but not something like that. And he wouldn't lie to you. Talk to Salem about it when he gets back."

"Back from telling his girlfriend he's dutybound to marry me? That sucks! That's where he is now, you know. Justice told me. Said he claims he's checking on the north border, but really he goes off to visit her instead."

I have no idea what she's talking about, but I intend to get to the bottom of whatever makes her look so very despondent. When she's collected herself, we walk around the gardens, taking our time so she can touch every petal that strikes her fancy. At her first yawn, I'm judicious in calling it a night. I don't want her dragging tomorrow.

There aren't many people in the mansion. Most of the servants avoid the two of us like the plague, skittering away every time we turn down a hallway. Vera's the only one salty enough to stand her ground, as if we're some big threat. "I saw ye," she says with a sneer on her lips. "I saw ye cursing the ground out there!"

Lily stiffens, and I can feel her fear rising up that she'll be tried for something she can't possibly do. "I didn't do anything like that!"

"Stay out of my gardens, lass! Ye aren't welcome here."

I cluck my tongue at Vera. "Now, now. Is that any way to talk to Prince Salem's future bride?"

She shudders every time I mention that, which is like a gift that keeps on giving. I chuckle at her shiver of disgust and tip my imaginary hat to her as we keep moving down the hall, away from the confrontation.

My bedroom in Salem's mansion is the usual bare stone room, but I've got a stack of comic books on the bedside I refuse to be embarrassed by. Harris and Melinda never allowed such childish things at home, so Salem bought some for me years ago and stores them here for me to enjoy whenever I visit.

Lily lays down in her jeans and long-sleeved navy t-shirt, and it's then I realize she has nothing. My wife doesn't have a single possession in this land except the clothes on her back. The Princess of Drexdenberg doesn't have pajamas.

I keep a small stack of clothes here, and waste no time in pulling out my softest t-shirt and flannel pants. "These will be too big, but they've got to be more comfortable than what you've been traveling in."

"Thanks. That's real nice of you." She fingers the material, and I'm instantly ashamed. She's impressed by flannel. My wife thinks men's pajamas are a brilliant gift.

"You deserve better than that. I'll make sure you get what you need in the morning."

She turns the pants over in her hands. "I've got you," she says simply. "What more could there be?"

"So much more," I promise.

Though we've not traded more than kisses, I don't want it to always be that way. So I make the decision not to leave for the bathroom to get changed for bed. My jeans and shirt come off and puddle on the floor while she watches me with curious eyes.

11

HOME AWAY FROM HOME

DESTINO

"Has no man ever changed in front of you before, or are you looking at me like that because you're just that enthralled with my body?" I love teasing a blush out of her, though it might not be the best time for such things. Then again, perhaps I'm the perfect distraction from her melancholy. The shock of pink on those pale cheeks is just about the best sight in the world. So many things are shared between me, Alex and Salem, but that blush is only for me.

My eyes are glued to her form when she slowly slides her shirt over her head. I should watch and enjoy the show from where I am so I don't spook her, but I can't stay away. My feet move on their own, closing the gap between us in three long strides. She squeaks against my lips when my mouth crashes on hers, but she doesn't pull back. Her fingers dig into my bare uninjured shoulder, pressing her breasts against me while I topple us backwards onto the bed with her atop me. We make quick work of tearing her jeans down her legs. Her skin against mine is just about the best feeling in the world, so I wrap her around me in every way I can, cocooning myself in her body.

Her lips are so soft, her skin perfumed with her natural lily and peach scent. Everything about her is a gift that slowly unravels the more I stroke and tease the tantalizing parts of her. I want exactly this, only this, and finally it's just us. I can enjoy the woman I've been rapidly growing addicted to. I can take my time exploring her skin. Her flesh seems to glow with its own light that always guides me to safety. To the edge of danger. To where I belong.

She's desperate for connection tonight, clinging tight to my body while we roll around in the sheets. It's like she's afraid if she lets go, she'll be swept away into some abyss. She thinks I won't be able to find her there, but I will. I can always find her. I snatch her lower lip between my teeth and pull, drawing a moan from her as her uninjured leg loops around mine. I love that she lets me touch her tender skin with my fangs, that she's not afraid of me.

But she is afraid of something. She's unable to relax, kissing me frantically like she's trying to run from the phantom thing that's chasing her. "Hey," I say as my lips drag down her throat. I can't help my groan when she arches atop me. "It's alright. We've got all night. I'm not going anywhere."

That tips it. Whatever she was running from finally catches her, choking a tearless sob from her lips. She's horrified at the sound. Her whole body stiffens and she covers her face with her hands to hide her shame from me. "I'm sorry!"

Though I want nothing more than to ignore the things that might put a stop to this moonlit moment, her agony takes top billing and slows my seduction. "Blue eyes, what's wrong?" My lips move to her forehead, and though I have no plans to leave my spot beneath her nearly-naked form, the frantic nature of our connection turns tender as I run my finger over the apple of her cheek.

She shakes her head and tries to smile through what clearly looks to me like devastation. "Nothing at all. I'm glad you're not going anywhere. I like you right here." Her fingers glide over my thigh and then dig into the muscles, exciting my body to keep me from her heart. She's playing dirty, hiding in plain sight on this precipice of bravery and cowering. But words turn into throaty moans of pleasure as she massages tension out of me I didn't realize I had. I mean to tell her I love her, but I'm not sure she understands how significant that is.

Lily is limber and lean, which means when she straddles me, her long legs coil in ways a man can't ignore. My good hand slides down her side, giving her shivers that drive her pelvis to rock atop mine. I want her so very badly, but our first time shouldn't be outlined in worry, which I can still see tightening the corners of her eyes.

I flick her hip to stop her manic makeout. Then I roll to my right, dumping her beside me so I can nuzzle her nose as the lantern flickers on the far wall. There are just enough shadows on her face to keep me guessing, but the fragmented slivers of light let me know she needs more than just my body right now.

She needs *me*.

"Easy, Lil," I say as our kisses slow into a languid and luxurious connection. It's my turn to massage her, so I reach around for her butt. I love that she lets me loop my fingers under the lacy material so I can get that much closer to her. "You're worried," I observe. "Talk to me."

"You don't want to hear it." She kisses me harder in an effort to run from the conversation. "I don't want to feel it. Don't make me say it."

"Say what?"

"That I'm afraid. I don't want to be afraid. I'm in bed with you. I just want to be here."

I rub the wrinkle between her eyebrows. "I'll still be just as lust-worthy tomorrow. What are you afraid of?"

She shivers, and I curse myself for not remembering how cold this place is in comparison to what her body was made for. I reach down and roll awkwardly to use my good arm to tug the comforter up over us, rubbing warmth into her spine under the covers. It's as simple as that to get her to stop running and really lean into me. Her chilly fingers creep up the side of my neck. They feel small, and as she burrows into my chest, so does she. In this enormous mansion, it's just the lantern and the two of us, hiding under the covers like children who have nothing but each other when the monsters under the bed come to snap at our ankles. She's dainty in a way that suddenly seems breakable, so I remind myself to be the best kind of gentle with all the parts of her she's entrusted to me.

Her leg stays looped around my hip, her lace-clad breasts pressed to my chest when she finally unburdens herself of all that's been keeping her on edge. "It was a bear," she confesses in a gust of angst. "A shifter bear who scarred my face. He was just a cub, but so was I back then. I was so scared. Even after Fiora took me in, I had night-mares for years."

I want to kick myself for not putting that together sooner. Of course she'd be anxious in the place she was abandoned, dumped and then attacked. "I can imagine." I kiss her nose and keep my body tight to hers, cupping her butt and thumbing the swell I covet above all else.

"I'm nervous here. I don't want to be, but I can't help it. I'm not supposed to be afraid of people I don't know, people who've done nothing wrong to me, but I keep checking over my shoulder all the time, waiting for that bear to finish the job." She shakes her head. "That sounds silly."

"No, it doesn't. It sounds like you're very brave to be here. You should've told me you were this frightened. I took you outside to see the gardens. I wouldn't have done that if I knew it made you uneasy."

"Everything makes me uneasy when we're apart. We weren't meant to be separated, the four of us. I broke us."

I kiss her lips once to remind her that not everything is broken. "One time when we were younger and figuring out how to hold on to each other while our territories were at war, we split like this. Salem's people attacked the fae, and Alex took it to heart. Said he wouldn't come back to us until the shifters were on their own soil again. We break on occasion," I admit, thumbing her butt beneath the lace. I love this bit of her. "It's part of being as close as we are, and carrying the weight we do. This isn't on you. Alex gets touchy sometimes. He likes to be the swindler, not the one getting swindled." When she flinches at my words, I kiss her nose. "It's okay, blue eyes. We only just met a couple months ago. I don't expect you to tell me your darkest secrets in so short a time. Alex will come around. Sometimes you have to give someone the time to ease into something that they didn't grant you."

She doesn't cry, instead trusting me to hold her together while she teeters on the edge of falling apart. "Salem has a girlfriend," she whispers. "I feel so icky and stupid. I thought… I'm younger than I realized, I guess, believing in first kisses and true loves and all that. This entire time, he's had a girlfriend."

I truly have no idea what Justice is on about, telling Lily something as daft as that. "I'll sort it all out in the morning. There is no other woman. I don't know why Justice would say that to you, other than to drive you away."

"Then where is Salem?" Of course, she asks the one thing I don't know. Git's been gone ever since supper ended. "I shouldn't have pushed him about asking me to marry him. Why did I say that?"

"Because you're a grown woman who wants to be treated like one. You did nothing wrong or even all that risky. Salem needed the sharp slap of reality. For all his brains on the battlefield, he has no idea what he's doing with women."

"Then where is he?"

"Salem stepped out for a while, is all. He's been away from Jacoba for weeks, blue eyes. He's the commander of the shifter army. He's got to check in, do his job. I know he wanted to make sure your father was properly locked up and all, too. And if he says he's checking on the northern border, then that's where he is."

"This is the closest I've lived to my father since I was a child." She shivers against me, and my stupid right arm can do nothing about it, useless as it is, so I run my left hand up and down her bicep. "I don't like it."

My hand drifts lower and coils around her butt protectively. I love this part of her. "I don't like it, either." I adore the way her skin feels against mine. Like I'm her warm thing when life threatens to turn her cold. "Tell me more."

"I know it's irrational, but I keep worrying that at any moment, the bear cub from sixteen years ago is going to come bursting through that door. Then the second I talk myself out of that, the image of General Klein barreling through to steal me away from my home bombards me."

My lips curve up in half a smile. "See? That's progress. You're thinking of this place as your home."

She shoots me a wry look laced with attitude. "That's only because you're here."

My chest expands with pride. "One day, those fears will get smaller. Until then, I'm right here."

"It's not this place," she tells me, snuggling in closer. "It's you. *You're* my home, Des."

Her declaration floods me with pride that's mixed with a peace I didn't realize I'd been lacking. My lips find hers, indulging in the long and luxurious kiss we both need. "Then I'll make sure no one takes you away from me," I promise.

I leave her only long enough to lock the door and slide the chest of drawers in front of it. I'm not worried about anything coming in the night, but the second I take her fears seriously, I see her relax against the pillow.

"That should do it. Now we can get some sleep."

Lily's nearly naked form curls around mine, and if there's an inch between us, I don't feel it. My hips are married to hers, her leg over my waist to claim my body. Her breasts are nestled to my chest, and when her lashes finally flutter shut, my heart promises her things in the dark that I know will hold true in the daylight.

As long as I'm around, my wife will be safe.

12

A MOTHER'S ADVICE

ALEXAVIER

How I became the heavy drinker in the group, I'll never know. Ever since Lily came around, Des doesn't get drunk nearly as much. Yet here I am, downing my fifth cocktail of the night because my vision's started to clear.

I don't want to see things unblurred. They sting too badly, and there's no end in sight. I slouch in my ivorum chair on the balcony, replaying all the reasons I'm angry with Lily, because I keep forgetting them the lonelier I get for her. For all of them, really. The guys and I rarely fight, but when we do, it feels like this—hollow and sad with a note of dread. I've learned most of those things can be cured with alcohol, but today my melancholy is only made worse by the stuff.

"You should slow down, Alexavier," Mother says as she joins me on the balcony, sitting a few feet away in the spare chair. She's a much more graceful drunk than I am. Then again, she's got more practice with the art. "Whatever you're running from, you can't outdrink it."

I scoff. "You're one to talk."

Mother's eyes cut to me. "Then learn from my experience. I'm still your mother."

"You let Father talk about my wife like she's beneath us. You knew he never intended on letting us marry. If saying nothing is being my mother, then you're an excellent one, that's shore sure." Yeah, I'm an ass when I'm drunk, especially when I slur my words without meaning to.

Mother goes silent, which is worse than being yelled at. I'm being Father to her, running her down because she says things I don't like. I shut her up with my words, just like him.

"I shouldn't have said that," I admit, rubbing my forehead.

She reaches over the divide between us and jerks the tumbler from my hand. "Amateur. You handle your liquor like a schoolboy." She downs my glass in one swallow, to which I applaud, because I'm just that drunk. "I married an ass, but I'll be damned if I raised one as well." She holds up the glass and taps it with her painted fingernail. "So tell me, to what are we drinking on this fine evening?"

"To the end of my marriage!" I slap on a grin filled with malice and slide the flask from my pocket, toasting her empty glass with it.

I expect her to relax at the news and maybe even chuckle, but she sits up straight, her mouth firm with disapproval. "What did you do?"

I scoff. "I love that you assume I'm to blame. Lily lied to me." I wait for the big ah-ha moment where Mother takes back her assumption that it's all my fault, but it never comes.

"So? How many lies have you told this week?"

"Hardly any at all. That's not the point. Lily lied to me. *Me.*"

"Why did she lie to you?"

It's not the question I anticipate, so for a second, I'm stumped. "She did something terrible, and never told me about it. Something so bad, I can't get past it. But it's not what she did; it's that she hid it from me."

"Why did she lie to you?" Mother repeats, as if the question is worth saying a second time.

"Lily should've trusted me. She should've come clean and told me everything. I deserve to know who I'm marrying!"

"Did I deserve to get cut out of my son's wedding?"

"What? We're not talking about that. It's neither here nor there. Lily and I did what we had to."

"Did I deserve it?"

I slump back in my seat and take another glug from my flask. "I suppose not. I was livid with Father, not you. I suppose you want me to apologize?"

She's quiet for a moment. So quiet, I'm worried that maybe I've gone too far and truly hurt my own mother, whose biggest mistake today was coming out to sit with her prick of a son. "What I want is for you to be happy. Answer me, Alexavier. Why did Lilya lie to you?"

I stare at the moon, which looks larger than usual. It's peaceful, reminding me that I am not. It mocks me, and I have no choice but to let it look down on me like it knows best. I chew on my lower lip as I mull over Mother's question she won't stop asking. "Lilya lied because she accidentally did something horrible, and she didn't want me to hate her for it. How could she think so little of me?"

"Well, how did you handle it when she came clean?"

"I ended things."

Mother takes my flask and pours some into the glass she's stolen from me. "Smart girl, then. One lie to cover over an accident, and her marriage gets jerked out from under her. Best she gets out now before she falls too hard for you."

I balk at my mother, who's finally got something to say. "I beg your pardon? You're glad it's over for *her* sake? You're happy for *her*?"

"Wouldn't you be? To think, a marriage can end the week it begins because a woman says something that displeases the crown."

The way Mother says "the crown" sounds like she's making fun of me, like I'm snooty and think I'm above Lilya. Nothing could be further from the case. "Lilya lied to me."

"And you kicked her out. Where is she staying?"

I shrug, and the first pangs of dread fight through the alcohol to twist at my stomach. I should've asked where she'd be staying. "Probably with Salem in Jacoba."

"Probably?" Mother sits up straighter, as if she's grown

a spine out of thin air. "Your family lies once, and you don't even care enough to make sure they've got somewhere safe to sleep? You sent her off with a shifter? I didn't know you had such cruelty in you, Alexavier."

"Cruelty? I sent her off with Salem and Destino. That's hardly cruel."

"And where are they staying?"

"I told you, I don't know. Probably in Jacoba."

"After what her face looks like? A shifter scarred her, Alexavier! You abandoned her to a man who had no choice but to take her back into shifter territory? The place she barely escaped alive when she was a girl?" It's then I see Mother's truly angry at me, hurt that I'm disappointing her grand expectations that I not end up like...

Dread washes over me. Am I like my father?

Mother's tone calms, but there's a deadly disapproval that coats every word. "I'm so glad you brought her here, announced her to the whole of Faveda as your wife, and then deserted her, sending one of our own off into shifter territory. If there was ever any doubt that you're your father's son..."

"Don't say it," I warn her through gritted teeth. "Lilya will be safe with Salem."

"Until she tells Salem her dirty secret, that is. Then will he kick her out as well?"

My mouth goes dry. Guilt so powerful that even alcohol can't subdue it crashes into me. "He knows. So does Des. She told us together."

The silence that falls between us says a great many

things. Mother lets my conscience fill in the gaps for a solid minute before she speaks. "Then I'm glad she escaped you. She deserves to be happy after what her father put her through. Salem and Destino actually care about her."

"I care about her, Mother."

"No, you care about yourself. You care about being right. About winning the argument. You put your sore feelings above her actual safety. If I raised you at all, I see no traces of it now." She stands and takes my flask. "Your father can have you."

Then my mother leaves me with the torrent of worry that comes from second-guessing myself. She walks slowly with her head high, and though I'm angry with her for bringing up too many valid points, I realize my mother finally spoke for herself, and I couldn't be more proud of her for the victory.

It takes me an entire five minutes before I move into the palace and trip down the hallway to my mother's bedroom. "Mother, I shouldn't have..." But I'm not sure what I'm seeing when I open her door. "Are you going somewhere?"

Mother straightens, and then shoves a stack of folded clothing in to an overnight bag. "My daughter-in-law sent word from Jacoba this morning, asking the rulers to meet to discuss future plans for peace between the territories."

"You knew that's where she was?"

"Yes. I wanted to see if *you* knew who was looking after your wife. Lilya wants to talk strategy for unification, so that's where I'm headed."

"It's not going to work. Father wants nothing of the sort."

"Your father didn't get a chance to read the note. I intercepted it, so I'm taking myself a little vacation. I might happen by the mansion in Jacoba, and I might happen to sign whatever peace agreement I'm presented with."

My whole body comes to life at the prospect of my mother involving herself in what can only be described as espionage of the highest degree. "You can't do that, Mother. Father will never go along with it."

"I think you're forgetting, as your father often does, that I'm the Queen of Faveda. My signature is just as binding. It's only your perception of my power that's weak, not my power itself."

"How much have you had to drink today?" I ask slowly, wary of something I never saw coming.

The first sign of nerves gives my mother a shiver, but she doesn't back down. "Not nearly enough, but I suppose I should be mildly clearheaded when I go to a meeting with King Ronin, my daughter, and the Butcher boys."

My head turns slowly from left to right, but even as I think up reasons why she shouldn't go against my father in such a big way, the prospect of it excites me. "Maybe I should go with you. Be your escort."

Mother sniffs in my direction. "I'll not put Lilya through having to see your face. You betrayed her. You're a boy with a pout. She's a woman with a plan."

I take two steps into her room, my twisting stomach finally settling the moment I make the decision I know I'll never be able to undo. I may not be ready to see Lilya, but I know I need to. I want to. "Then I should bring her flowers. Apologies always go better when there's a gift involved."

Mother lifts her chin. "I suppose I can't stop you from trying to rectify the utter mess you've made of the best thing that ever happened to you." Insecurity flashes in her blue eyes. "Quickly, Alexavier. Pack your bag and meet me in secret in the stables. I'll be gone in five minutes, with or without you. If your father finds out, I will be punished most severely."

I reach out and hold my mother's hand, only to find it's trembling. "He won't stop us. And when we come back, you'll stay with Lilya and me, so you'll never have to look at father's face again."

She closes her eyes, and for a second, I'm concerned she might cry. "I love you, my boy. Let's go change the world."

13

MOTHER AND BROTHER

LILYA

It's five days since Salem left, and I've given up hope there can be anything good that comes from this. I don't want to pine, but stuck indoors as I am, there's precious little else for me to do.

Ronin will be here tonight. It's my one shining thought that keeps me from slipping into dark places in my mind. I called a meeting of the rulers, since apparently, that's something I'm allowed to do. If we want a real shot at peace, we have to actually all be able to sit in a room together and plan for it.

I make my way down to Queen Butcher's room while Des is having his daily visit from Healer Wesley down the hall to try and fix his arm. It's my daily habit, sitting on the floor with my back leaning against her tall bedside. I open the copy of the history of Jacoba and rest it on the stone floor. I read it aloud to Queen Butcher, who doesn't judge me for the remedial education I never had the opportunity to further. I pretend she's my mother who listens and smiles at me even when I stumble over words every ten-year-old knows. I study daily, willing myself not to get frustrated or overwhelmed. Even if Salem is only marrying me because he wants peace in the land, I'm still responsible to care for the shifters. I can't very well do that if I don't know who they are or where this great people came from.

I can't stand the stench of the incense that hovers in the air in this small space. The sandalwood pierces my nose in ways that stay with me hours after I'm gone from this room.

I'm freezing. Always freezing. The stone surfaces offer no heat or cushion, so it is what it is. The rooms and hallways are drafty, and when the wind blows, I feel the howl and bite of the breeze that makes me shudder.

When the door opens, I jump, but my shoulders lower when Justice enters. "Ye always look like someone's about to attack ye whenever you're startled. Thought I might find ye here."

"Did you need something?"

"Lots of somethings," he admits with a tired smile. He does that a lot, smiles in a way that makes it look like he's forgotten how, but it's still buried deep inside of him somewhere just out of reach. "Salem sent word tha he's at the barracks and taking care of some personal matters. He'll be back in a few days."

I nod, accepting with a grimace the salty pill that Salem sends messages he's too busy to tell me himself. He's gone, and I'm the afterthought. I'm only here because of him, and now I'm stuck in this freezing house, trying to figure out why and where I'm supposed to belong.

"Doing a bit of light reading, I see. It's decent of ye to come read to my mammy. I admit I'm not the incredible son I used to fancy myself. It's hard to be in this room. See her here, but not." His eyes flit to the thick, worn book sitting on the floor before my crossed legs. "I can get ye a tutor, if ye like."

I stiffen. "What do you mean?"

He runs his hand over his face, looking very much like Salem. "I mean, I listen in on ye from time to time, and I hear ye stumbling over words. They don't have schools in Neutral Territory. Did ye drop out before ye got shipped there?"

"I was eight," I tell him, unwilling to go more into the story I loathe.

The silence that hangs between us is thick with his unasked questions. I'm on my guard against them, which I'm guessing he can sense, because the only thing he mutters is, "General Klein's a mangey bastard for abandoning his daughter there so young. Ye only know the worst parts of us, having grown up in Neutral Territory. Let me get ye a tutor."

I do my best to iron out the attitude I feel flaring, offering him a polite head-tilt. "I highly doubt any of your people are going to be thrilled to educate a fae. I can read just fine. You can do all sorts of things without an education."

"Fair point. You've proved tha." His eyes flick to the

text. "It's been a long day, and it's not even noon. I hate tha ye asked for a meeting of the rulers. They'll be here soon, and I'm already on edge."

I'm not thrilled when he lowers himself to sit beside me, but he does it anyway.

I flip the page and scowl at the words, so I don't accidentally glare at Justice. "Stinking Territorials. Get used to working together. Solving your lands' problems on your own has never worked. You all have me in common now, whether you like it or not. Ronin's great." I ignore Justice's huff of disbelief. "King Fairbucks is awful, granted, but he won't always be on the throne. Your people are going to die if they don't get fresh water. The only way to make that happen is by lowering the borders."

He leans his head against the side of the mattress. It's a little comical, a prince sitting on the floor like this. He sighs loudly. "Read to me? Tha might calm my nerves about this whole thing."

I'm nervous now. Queen Butcher doesn't correct me or huff when I get something wrong. Of course, she *can't* do any of that, but I get to pretend I'm smart enough to impress her by my epic out-loud reading. Justice, on the other hand, hasn't held back his opinions about me, reminding me daily how I very much don't belong here, and that I will not be a good match for his brother. There isn't aggression to his honesty, which I guess is good, but as my eyes skim the first line when I pick up the book, my palms begin to sweat.

"'1864 – The Year of the Cashing Mo-moun-moun-

mountain.'" I sound like an idiot. This will be the thing that seals it. He'll know for sure I'm not good enough for his brother now.

Justice looks over my shoulder and nods. "'Crashing,'" he corrects me, not unkindly.

"Right. 'The Year of the Crashing Mountain. In the fourth month, Stephen Pruitt, a fae, crossed over into Jacoba. In an effort to take out the shifter people, he soug? Soft?"

"Sought," Justice says. This time he takes my finger and traces the letters in the middle. "Tha's a confusing word to sound out. Makes more sense the way ye said it."

He takes my finger and covers up the middle letters this time, so I can see the word as it's meant to be pronounced.

"He sought to bring Mount Prowl down on our heads. Thirty shifters were killed in the avalanche, twelve injured. A law was enacted that no home should be built within fifty yards of a mountain hencef...hence..."

"Henceforth. Tha's a stuffy word tha means from now on."

I fight the urge to tell him I know what 'henceforth' means; I just don't know how to spell or read it. Instead, I point to the text. "Does this get amended later on? The rule isn't still like this, is it?"

Justice sighs. "I know ye don't like to think the fae are capable of mass-murder, but it's true. We keep laws in place tha make sure shifters live to see another day."

I shake my head, swallowing my confession that he's sitting right next to a fae mass-murderer. "It's not that.

This isn't enough distance from the mountain, is all. Fifty yards will work fine for your average fae with a vendetta, but if you get one that's gifted, that's not enough space."

Justice's eyebrows knit together. He inches closer to peer at the text. "How much space? If we're contemplating lowering our border walls and inviting the enemy in, we need to be prepared for stuff like this."

"You're not inviting the enemy in. If you do, that's all you'll get. You're inviting new friends in. It's all in how you view it. You set the tone as their leader."

"I won't say it to them like tha."

"You think shifters are stupid enough not to spot a lie? Maybe I think more of your people than you do." I shake my head at him.

Of all things, Justice chuckles at me. "Then what do ye propose, wee ruler?"

"Moving people out of the homes that are too close to the mountain, for one. And at some point, it would be nice to see a map of Jacoba. Then we can ask strategically for what we want from the fae, instead of just taking whatever they give us."

"I guess I didn't think of tha. I don't have as much faith as ye do in us coming together."

"Then let's plan. How many plumapples are you willing to part with?"

Justice's eyebrows raise. "Already negotiating, are we?"

"We have strengths. Even though we don't have enough water, we're not without assets."

"Ho, it's 'we' now, is it? You're an honorary shifter, are

ye, wee mongrel?" He grins, and for a second, I forget that he doesn't want me near his brother. He looks at me like we might be alright someday when the dust on all this unorthodox change settles.

"That's right. My animal is whatever scares irritating wolves into playing nice."

His chest vibrates as he gets up and fishes around in the nightstand drawer. He pulls out a pencil and parchment, spreading it out on the floor. He narrates his drawings as he lays out the whole of Jacoba for me in squiggles and lines, telling me where the larger populations of people reside, where the ground needs the most work, and any giant obstructions, like mountains or steep canyons.

"How many wells would you want near the main village? Maybe six?" I suggest, and he draws six circles. "But you want growth for the kingdom. It's not good for shifters to be all crowded on top of each other. Many of them probably prefer rural settings. Let's have a dozen more further out, so there's room for the population to explode."

Justice's eyes tighten. "Population's been declining for years. I think the vampires and fae would be happy to see us snuffed out."

He's not wrong, from what I've witnessed. However, I address his first concern to start. "That sort of thing happens when resources are scarce and the people are worried. Besides, the worst that happens is you have too many wells." I don't know why I feel like it might be okay for me to reach across the space between us and pat the top of his hand. I'm shocked he doesn't jerk away. "Not all of us want to see the shifters gone. I need someone to believe it's not hopeless. Maybe hope should start at the top, with the leaders." I swallow hard. "When Salem was beaten up for his peace walk through vampire territory, he wasn't alone. There were a few shifters with him. They believe."

"Aye," Justice allows. "But tha's shifters. We're going to lower our borders to people who want us gone."

My voice goes quiet, bouncing off the stone walls and coming back in whispers. "When Des did his peace walk through shifter territory, he wasn't alone either. He went with a few vampires who all believe. And your people beat them badly. For walking. The day I married my husband, he had a black eye and a broken arm. Look the other way all you want, but I want more for them than that. You should, too. If their leader doesn't believe there's something better out there, then you're leading them nowhere."

Justice goes still for several beats, and I know I've overstepped. When his thumb finally sweeps over my knuckles, I relax a little. "Is this what it's like to have a sister? I admit, I'm not sure I like being told I'm imperfect. At least Salem has the sense to keep his gob shut and plan massive catastrophes behind my back."

I manage an airy snigger. "I've never had a brother before. I'll make sure to keep you on your toes."

"Grand. Do ye know how to fence, wee bunneh?"

I snigger at the way the word "bunny" sounds on his tongue. The shifter accent is completely adorable. "Fencing? That's for like, fancy people. I do okay with my dagger."

He tsks me. "But you're a princess now. Fencing is more dignified. I could teach ye, if ye like."

The note of a peace offering hangs in the air, so I take it. "That might be nice. Thanks."

He stands and pops open the window overlooking Queen Butcher's bed. "It's been ages since I've aired out this room. The sandalwood's a bit much."

I shiver at the icy breeze, but I'm grateful for the scents of the outdoors. My heart aches every time nature is near, but not close enough to touch. How I wish I wasn't a blight on the gift of the fae.

Justice plops back down beside me but doesn't make eye contact, instead studying a scuff on his knuckles. "Ye were up last night, walking the halls."

I keep my gaze on the book. "Is there a question layered in that, an accusation, or just an observation?"

"I guess all three." He holds his hand out and tilts it from side to side. "Maybe less of an accusation than there would've been a week ago. You're growing on me, more than I would've guessed."

"Must be hard to be wrong. That's gotta hurt. You want to lie down?"

He elbows me through a snigger, which is progress, to say the least. "Aye, it is hard. My pride's delicate, I'll have ye know."

I feign shock. "No, you?" I feel my spine relaxing, my whole body forfeiting a portion of my unease, now that we're getting along.

"Hush your gob, wee pup. I'm trying to apologize."

"Are you working your way up to it?"

"Jays, woman. I'm sorry, okay? I didn't give ye a chance. I was shortsighted."

I pat him atop the head, earning a grin that makes him look boyish, like a brother should. "There, that wasn't so difficult. I forgive you for being a tool."

He scoffs. "I'm not so sure how I feel about having a sister who calls me a tool."

"Lucky for me, you don't get a choice in the matter."

Justice scoots closer, this time with only a foot of space between us. "Read to me? I can't get out of my head."

"Too much on your plate, or too much on your mind?"

He lets out a one-noted snort. "Maybe a little of both. This marriage thing is… I'm still sorting it out."

"Me too," I admit. "It seemed a whole lot simpler before you told me about Salem's girlfriend. I don't mind pissing off the world so they move toward a better future, but stealing another woman's man? That's just plain mean. I don't want to be that girl."

Justice doesn't tell me what to do. He says nothing, which, as it turns out, is the exact right thing to say.

So I read to him. My new brother. When I can't figure out a word, he takes my finger and points it to the letters while he helps me sound it out. He doesn't look at my face or make any sign that he's exasperated with my limited education. Every now and then, he reaches behind him and touches his mother's hand, a glassy look in his eyes while he listens to the annals of kings passed.

The historical language soothes us, taking us to a time when things felt equally doomed as they do now, I'm sure, but somehow they got through it. It gives me hope that one day, we'll be able to write down that we got through this harrowing journey as well.

He's not listening anymore, which is just as well. I'm making a mess of the text. I'm fairly certain King Paul III didn't *decaffeinate* seven people who stood up against his rule. Justice closes his eyes, and I can't tell if he's overwhelmed or just plain exhausted by life. After a few more minutes, the steady rhythm of his breathing soothes me enough to put down the book.

I haven't been sleeping well. I made ugly cookies for Des so he could have good dreams at night, but I don't want any part of them. Though, this is probably the one time in my life I truly need a rest from my nightmares. The shifter bear from my childhood greets me every time I close my eyes. Only in my nightmare, he's clawing not just at my face, but at my arms, my chest, my back, my legs—all of me is shredded by the time I wake.

Ugly cookies laced with the eevana leaves give a person happy dreams, but I don't want the lie. I want to face my fears instead of bury my head in the sand. I want to fight back against that bear, but I'm paralyzed to defend myself. Still, each night I go back into the ring, ready to go another round with my demons.

Salem's not here. I don't know how safe we are. I still

haven't convinced myself that bear cub won't come for me in the daylight, ready to take a swipe at my other cheek. But listening to Justice's calm in and out makes my eyelids feel heavy. I'm not part of their family, but I pretend for just a little bit that I am. That my mother, brother and I stayed up late reading, and then we fell asleep because all our bills are paid, all our cupboards are full, and all our worries are small.

I don't know why I trust Justice not to attack me in my sleep. Maybe because he's been so open about his disdain for me joining his family. There's something comforting about outright disapproval. I prefer it to false kindness. And it seems he's too nice a guy to maintain his grudge against me, which suits us both just fine.

I curl up a few feet from Justice and rest my head on the stone floor. I'm freezing, but the constant shivering has worn me out.

When my eyes close, the room is quiet and peaceful. When they open however long later, it's to the crack of something hard across the side of my head.

14

THE MATE BOND

SALEM

I felt it. Something. Something hit me, but it didn't. I turn back to the structure tha's not nearly as far along as it needs to be. It's got four walls, sure, but not much else. I should've had some of the soldiers help me with it, but tha didn't sit right. If they installed a beam incorrectly, it could fall on Lily and crush her. I can't chance it.

I've been away for too long. I can feel it. I didn't want to leave in the first place, but I had to. Lily wanted a proper proposal, which isn't a ridiculous thing for her to ask. I'm the thick-headed idiot who didn't think it through. I didn't treat her like a treasure. I treated her like a convenience. I'll get better at this, starting with this next support beam tha's... This is going to take forever. On top of the fact tha I've had to spend my evenings at the barracks, checking in on my captains and making sure they didn't let the place fall apart in my absence.

A week without Lily feels like the worst kind of punishment, but I know I deserve it for not being the man she deserves. Des promised to look after her, so she should be fine.

Another invisible bash to my temple hits me so hard, it makes me flinch. It takes me a few minutes of looking around and shaking it off to realize tha nothing hit me.

I'm instantly sick to my stomach when I realize the phantom fight isn't directed at me at all: it's meant for Lily, and I'm feeling the pangs of it through our bond.

Panic slices through me like lightning, and before I can put away my tools, my feet are carrying me toward the mansion. I don't have to will my wolf to burst out of me; he knows how to move faster than my two-legged self. The plot of land I picked isn't too far from the mansion, but right now it seems days away. She's scared. She's hurt.

The trees are a blur, my paws swallowing the ground tha separates me from my mate. Another bash, this time against my side. I whine, not for my pain, but because if Lily's hurt, I'm in agony. Where is Des? Is he down, too?

It takes me far too long to get home, my erratic heart beating louder in my ears the closer I get to Lily. I don't bother turning into a man and calling out for her. I sniff the air for the scent of lilies and run. The stairs take me to Des' room, which irks me. My bedroom is bigger. She should be there so she can stretch out. I want my sheets smelling like her.

I stick my nose to the ground and follow the scent of Lily down to my mammy's room, where it's harder to pick out, even though the sandalwood stench is wafting out the open window. I hate tha stink, but Vera insisted it promotes circulation or healing or something like tha. My mammy's still in her coma, so the most the sandalwood's ever done is stink up her room.

Blood on the rug. There's blood on the rug. My entire being howls when my nose confirms tha it's my mate's blood. My mate and my brother. Two drip patterns.

In my haste to find my mate, I don't notice Des until he's nearly underfoot. I'm not sure if fury or fear hit me harder when I see Des is passed out, blood trickling from his nose. I turn back into my man form and slap my best friend's cheek until his eyes open.

"Help!" Des rasps, gripping my forearm with feeble fingers before his eyes roll back in his head.

"Aye, Des. I've got ye." I stand, hefting him up in my arms. He's a fair bit heavier than Lily, and my arms are sore from lifting beams all day. Still, my best friend needs me, so my body figures out how to help him. "You're too far from Lily. Which way?" I ask, taking a step further down the hall. He cries out like I'm actively driving a stake through his temple, so I head the other way. "I never thought I'd find a tracker more accurate than my nose, but your headaches are just the ticket today. Who has Lily? And where's Justice?"

I'm not sure Des can understand a word I'm saying. He looks delirious with pain as I run through the hallways with his head lolling over my forearm.

"Shite, whoever it is took her outdoors so ye couldn't

follow. I'll find her, Brother." We're still a few hours from sundown, so I set Des in the parlor and draw the shades. I bolt out the door, spotting a splash of blood on the stoop.

I take a long drag of the air, my heart stuttering when I pick out notes of Lily straight ahead. When my eyes fall on another splash of blood in front of the storm cellar a few yards away, all fear melts into pure fury. Someone's taken my mate underground. My mate and my brother.

My boots are heavy when I stomp through the yard, flinging open the horizontal double doors and skipping the staircase with a leap downward that announces my presence. I hope they hear me. I hope whoever it is…

I stop short. "Vera? Where's Lily? Who's taken her down here?"

My round-faced housekeeper pales at the sight of me. She's probably afraid I'll get taken down by whoever abducted Lily, Justice and her. I can't imagine who's powerful enough to get the drop on Justice, and who's stupid enough to kidnap my mate. Though, I haven't even told my own brother about tha development yet, so word hasn't exactly spread tha I'm mated.

Vera's too scared to answer, but I don't need a name yet as much as I need to find Lily. Lily's whimper hits my ears, and I'm pushing past Vera toward the sound of fear on my woman.

She's bleeding. Bleeding as she sits with her hands bound behind her back, tied to a beam with her sweet arse on the packed-mud floor. *On the floor.* Soft lavender hair matted on one side and stained with crimson. Her breathing is labored, and she's not sitting fully upright, but leaning toward the left, as if her ribs can't handle movement and need babying.

I want to tear the throat out of whoever did this. I want them to regret ever laying eyes on the most perfect clouds-sent beauty. Someone with a death wish damaged her for reasons tha can only amount to utter madness.

Her closed eyes flutter open the moment my hand finds its home and cradles her face. She gasps at the sight of me, and then panic rises in her eyes. "Settle, Lily. I'm here. I'll…"

She's trying to warn me of something, maybe tell me who attacked her.

Something hits me hard on the back of my head. The world explodes in bursts of stars tha frame the one face I've been missing. Lily's got red ribbons streaking the side of her face, which scares me more than whatever it is tha's attacked me.

I whirl around to face my assailant, my mouth falling open at Vera's wild eyes and tear-streaked cheeks. I'm too stunned to duck when she bashes me over the head once more with the business end of a shovel. *My* shovel. The one I use to dig trenches. I can't make sense of what I'm seeing. Why is Vera holding my shovel and looking like she's the one who hit me?

One more crack and my knees go out. The last sound I hear is Lily screaming.

15

VERA'S LOVE AND MADNESS

LILYA

It was Salem's voice that roused me, and I'm still not sure where I am or what's going on. All I know is that Vera knocked Salem out with the business end of a shovel, and now she's bound his hands behind his back with thick ropes. I struggle against my own bindings, but my wrists are secured behind my back. I glance around to take in my surroundings. It's freezing, and my teeth actually chatter in the light that's cast by a single lantern on the hook in the corner. Are we in a stable? Somewhere underground? Are we in Jacoba still? I can see my breath, it's so cold.

Salem's sprawled on the floor not far from where I'm sitting, barely upright. My big hero being furiously hogtied in the middle of the dirt-packed floor stirs something both feral and tragic throughout my insides. The sight breaks something precious in me, forcing me to acknowledge the very real fact that Salem is mortal, and capable of being bested. I've never felt more mated to him than I do now. Though the magic doesn't touch me in the same way it's awakened him, I feel connected to him in some unshakable way. My mate is knocked out, so part of me feels the pang of potential defeat.

When Vera follows my eyeline, she does me the courtesy of explaining. "In case ye get grand dreams of either of them coming to and shifting themselves free, think again. There's silver in these ropes. It won't hurt them like it would a vampire, but it'll stop them from shifting. Silver keeps a shifter's magic weak, so the boys won't be going nowhere. I just have to…" She swallows hard, and I can tell she hasn't thought this part through.

"What's the plan?" I ask her, my head dizzy. "You can't possibly want to kill them. You love the Butcher boys. You've been their mom while Queen Butcher's been sleeping."

She narrows her eyes at me. "I never wanted to kill them! It's ye who came into the picture and messed the whole territory. Polluting the throne, they are. If I hadn't seen it with my own two eyes, I never would've believed it. No boy of mine would be caught dead with a fae." Vera punctuates her hatred by spitting at me. Then her eyes fall to the left of where I'm tied on the floor, secured to a support beam. Her silver brows tent with sudden worry. "The plan wasn't to hit Justice. But I saw the two of ye sleeping next to each other, and I lost it. Now I've got to think. Maybe Justice didn't see me."

I can't tell if she's right or not, but that hardly matters. I turn my chin with great effort, angling my head to the side so I can see more of my surroundings. My head hurts so terribly that I nearly vomit with the slight movement.

Justice is bleeding from his temple, his jaw slack and eyes closed. Terror slices through my resolve to stay in control of myself. "Did you kill him? Did you kill Justice? No! You killed a man because I slept in the same room as him? That's who you are? Justice! Justice, wake up!"

"Poisoning your food didn't work!" she offers up like that's a valid excuse for bludgeoning a prince.

"What?" The room keeps tilting, giving me slices of clarity and then stealing it away as I fight to stay conscious.

"For a week, I've been slipping arsenic into your meals, but ye kept waking up without so much as a stomachache! How did ye manage tha?"

I don't tell her that poison doesn't work on me. I'm too dizzy to access my magic just yet. I'm a sitting duck, at the mercy of a madwoman who'd just as soon see the ruling family dead than let them wander anywhere near me. If I could work my hands free, I could stuff her mouth with so much poison, she'd never be able to draw breath again.

Salem wouldn't want that, but I'm beyond caring. I'm not a law-abiding Territorial. I'm from Neutral Territory, and that's how we do things. We don't have a justice system we hold faith in, so judgment comes at our own hands, which has always worked well enough for me.

I'm not good, like Salem, though I know he wants me to be.

My breath comes in ragged pants, each inhale aching

my ribs. "You have to let Justice and Salem go. Do you understand what you've done?"

"I'm saving Jacoba from fae infiltration, is what I've done! I heard your lies, telling Justice how grand it'll all be when the fae are let into our land like the locusts they are. Not to mention the parasites who feed on blood and darkness. Do ye have any idea how many shifter lives have been lost at the hands of vampires? I *had* to do what I did." She looks like she might be sick as she picks up the shovel once more. "I never had the stomach for this part. Every day, I picture ending Queen Butcher, but I can't manage it." She turns her gaze on me again, and I'm surprised to see genuine pleading shining through. "See? I'm not a criminal. I'm someone who loves their territory. I'm a patriot. A loyalist."

The room slants again, but I fight to stay coherent. She's got the shovel aimed at the back of Salem's head, so I scramble to find my words. "You... How... Why would you want to end Queen Butcher?"

"Her coma suffices."

I catch a glimmer of pride in the lift of Vera's thick chin. It's hard to swallow the dread that bubbles up from my belly. "You're the reason Queen Butcher can't rule? *You* put her into a coma? Why? How could you do that to her?"

Vera studies Salem's motionless form while gnawing on her lower lip. "She wanted to sign a treaty with Drexdenberg years ago. King Ronin was pushing for a no-tariff trade agreement or some nonsense. Like we're going to up and shake hands with the enemy. The whole thing made me sick. Takes a monthly dose of bella donna to keep her under, but it's worth it. Then *her* boys became *my* boys, as it should've been. *I* cook and clean for them. *I* took them to school. *I* made sure they brushed their teeth and bathed more than once a month. I was always their mammy! Then Salem up and turns soft, like her, offering to marry fae scum? Did he turn a deaf ear to everything I taught the lad?"

Just a little more time. I need to breathe deeper, but it's so very cold. My ribs ache at the slightest movement. My mind is still rattling all over the place, my eyesight going in and out of focus. I have to keep her talking. I have to stay conscious.

I want her dead, even if I'm supposed to want a fair trial and all that.

Justice isn't moving. Not even his chest. "Oh, Vera! Did you kill him? Justice isn't breathing! Justice!" I shout, the sound absorbing into the dirt-packed walls. He was going to teach me how to read better. He was going to show me how to fence like a fancy person. He's supposed to inherit the crown.

He's supposed to be my brother.

For all her devious plotting, Vera drops the shovel and runs to Justice, testing his pulse with worry that mirrors my own. Her exhale of relief comes far too late for my comfort level, but it's there all the same.

She doesn't want to kill the Butcher boys.

"Ye had me for a second." She stands, eyeing her shovel with loathing. Then she rolls her shoulders back, and I can tell she's made a decision. "But it's gone on long enough, this fragile hold on the throne they have. I've got plenty of arsenic. Enough for Queen Butcher and both her boys. No need for things to get messier than they already have. It's time this ended." She looks down in reverence. "It'll be quick." Then her eyes flash to me with purpose.

My throat constricts, and I know she's made up her mind. No amount of diplomatic discussion or pleading will convince her that I'm a person worthy of compassion, or even life.

She's sweating, even though it's got to be cold enough to frost. When she picks up the shovel and turns in my direction, I know my time is up. Though I've resented my twisted brand of magic my whole life, it's suddenly become my very best friend. I've loathed my darker side, but now I hope against all odds that it's there for me when I need it most.

Vera doesn't have the same hesitation in her grip when she approaches me. I'm not a person to her, and definitely not family. I'm scum, nothing but a nuisance to be taken out with the trash.

The urge to hyperventilate is strong, but I manage to keep my breath steady as the room tilts again. Though I can't feel my fingertips, I will my magic to fill them. With everything inside of me, I need to be my own magic, not anyone else's. I may not be good enough to graduate from school or bloom healing herbs, but stiff as my fingers are, I am the exact twist of magic this corner of the world needs in this moment. My light will not be snuffed out. I will not go quietly into the void. I will fight for the family who fought for me.

I don't want to become a bitter woman who takes life, as if it's all so simple a choice. Even though I'm not sure I believe in Salem's ideals, if I want to become a Territorial, I have to try. I cannot murder Vera, even though the urge is on the verge of growing stronger than I can resist.

If magic is what you make of it, then I will use everything I have to make sure the Butcher boys are saved. I'll invest my magic in rescuing, rather than destroying.

I choke out a triumphant cry as petals birth and trickle from my fingertips, scattering themselves on the floor behind me.

I sound just deranged enough to give Vera pause as she peeks around me to the silky purple petals that come to my rescue. I've always resented them, hated my darker parts, but in this moment, I love them, and I find the strength to hate myself a little less.

Vera's grip on the shovel tightens. "What the…"

The petals pour from my palms now, scattering like playing cards that are bent on winning with a losing hand.

Vera's shovel swings hard, cracking the side of my head with force that makes my teeth ring. I don't care. Even as the light fades from my eyes, I know I've won. Her hatred is strong, but my love is stronger.

Her shovel drops to the floor, and a handful of seconds later, so does Vera. Her slumped form is the last thing I see before my magic runs dry and the darkness takes me.

16

IN RONIN'S ARMS

LILYA

"*E*asy, now." The voice breaks the silence I've been swimming in, but the muffled male cadence is so tender, I forgive the intrusion. "I've got you, darling. Alexavier, if I pass out again, I swear."

The answering male voice sounds muffled, like he's speaking through a rag or his shirt sleeve. "You won't. I covered the petals with dirt. That should keep the poison from hitting you again."

Is that Prince Alexavier? It can't be. My brain hurts, so I'm hearing what I want to hear. I'm immediately angry with my brain for betraying me by playing the one voice that causes me more pain than getting bludgeoned with a shovel.

A female voice I sort of recognize floats over my head. "Easy, King Ronin. Maybe you should let the soldiers fetch her."

I can hear the tension in Ronin's tone as he speaks

through what sounds like gritted teeth. "She is my family, not some soldier's. I will not trust to soldiers what I can do myself. She has no cause to trust them. If she wakes up in a stranger's arms, I will have failed as her father and her friend. She will be my queen someday." He's struggling against something. I can hear the strain in his voice.

I'm jostled only slightly, but bile rises from my belly at the slightest movement. Ronin's cologne tickles my nose, and though I can't bring myself to open my eyes, my body curls toward the scent of protection.

"I'm here, darling. Everything's going to be alright."

I don't believe him, but enough of me wants to so very much that I let myself float in the lie that loves me and carries me through the den of horrors. I never want to go near this place again, so I trust the lie that tells me love will save the day, that fathers can be good, that life doesn't have to be this constant struggle.

When icy air blasts my body and makes my head spin, I cuddle in closer, as much as I'm able. I can't hear them anymore, but I know people are talking. I can detect a low murmur, the rumble of voices broken up by the sound of my name. Then the wind dies down a handful of minutes later, and I hear dress shoes echo off stone floors.

Mansion. We're in the mansion. I'm in Ronin's arms. Even if everything else has fallen apart, that's one glimmer of goodness I steal from the air and keep for myself. Ronin will keep me safe.

Where is Salem? Did anyone help Justice? Did Vera

escape? Fiora. I need Fiora. She would know what to do. I miss her so very badly.

Blankets wrap around me, but I'm too frozen through to feel their effect. It's all I can do to make sense of where I'm at. The voices around me are shouting something, and fingers pry at my head, which is the last thing I want someone to do.

"Help them," I manage, though I still can't bring myself to open my eyes.

"We got them out." Ronin's cadence finds me, and something about the control in his voice eases my worry by a necessary degree. If Ronin's not upset, maybe all the problems in the world are fixable. Maybe everything isn't broken after all.

Maybe Salem is okay. Maybe I'll get to keep my new brother, even if Salem goes back to his secret girlfriend. I want him to have that choice. I don't want someone so incredible to die underground at the hands of a madwoman.

Maybe life won't pull the rug out from under me all over again.

"Darling, look at me." I can hear Ronin's control begin to slip. "Can you open your eyes? Please open your eyes! Has Vera said anything yet? Who did this to the princess?"

It's an effort I'm not sure is worth it when I open my eyes and the room starts spinning. I latch onto hints of stone walls and a long desk in the corner before I shut my eyes again to fend off vomiting. I have no idea where I'm at. Somewhere in the mansion, I assume, but not a room I recognize.

"She's awake! Healer Wesley, don't bother with the others. Lilya's the priority! If she dies, the territories will never unite."

I'm not sure that's true, but when more fingers prod at my skull, I can't bring myself to say as much. My stomach heaves as the pain ramps up, my whole body contracting like it needs to purge all that's gone wrong inside of me. I manage a few words of warning before I'm rolled onto my side and a bowl is shoved under my chin.

"It's alright, darling. This will pass. You're safe now."

Safe.

Ronin's fingers are gentle as he gathers my hair in his fist while I vomit. When my stomach settles enough to let me view the world again, I soak in the compassion from his pretty eyes. There's not a hint of disgust. "My mom! I need my mom!" I cry out as tears leak from my eyes. I'm not sure if I'm crying from emotion, or from the pressure that's pushing at my insides while my stomach heaves. I don't care that I sound childish and probably pathetic. Fiora stayed with me each time I took someone's poison into my body. She put cool cloths on my forehead and sang to me. The world tried to splinter apart the harder I scrambled to hold onto it, but she remained calm.

"You, go to Neutral Territory and fetch the shifter healer Fiora. She lives in the west end near the pub. But don't call her a healer; she hates that. If anyone gives her trouble for stepping back onto shifter soil and violating her banishment, you're to tell them she's been granted temporary access to Jacoba so she can tend to the princess of Drexdenberg."

If more puke wasn't rocketing out of me, I would tell Ronin how much I truly do love him, how grateful I am for him and how scared I still am. "Mom!" I cry for her. I only use that label aloud when I'm desperate, and I fear that's who I've become—a woman desperate for some semblance of safety.

Then I shake my head. "No. Don't call for her. I don't want her to see me like this."

"Prideful," Ronin scolds me, but doesn't argue further.

I expect Ronin to back away, but he doesn't turn from me when I'm a shell of a person. Instead he holds me steady while my body does what it needs to.

This is what a dad should do. This is a parent.

"Don't leave me," I beg Ronin, and I know I've passed my last vestiges of pride miles ago.

"Never," Ronin promises. Even if he's lying, I don't care. I'll take the lie and count it as kindness.

He holds my hair until I have nothing more in me to give. Then he hands me a cup of apple cider vinegar to gargle and spit out to clean my mouth and throat.

"There you are. Let's lie you down now. The healer can give you a look while we're fetching your mum, yes?"

"Don't leave," I say again, unsure if he took my worry seriously.

The usually hardened or cocky edges of his eyes soften with something that looks like compassion and perhaps even familial love. "We've already established I'm not leaving your side. I'll be right here until we leave for Drexdenberg, where I'll make sure nothing like this ever happens to you again."

I can only allow myself a solitary exhale before another worry takes me over. "I can't protect them yet. Watch them. Are they alive?"

"Yes, they're alive. We carried Destino upstairs so he could rest. Something about passing out from a headache? I've never heard such a thing from him before, but he was so bad off, he couldn't stand. Bloody nose. I'm not sure what to make of it. The healer gave him something to sleep it off; he was so delirious from the pain. Fought us on it. Said he needed to be near you." I somehow find the wherewithal to focus in on Ronin's teasing smirk.

"Where am I?" I ask as Healer Wesley comes into view. He dabs at the side of my head, tsking me for looking at the rag that comes away bloody.

Ronin's mouth tightens. "You're in Jacoba. Do you know your name?"

"Where in the mansion is Des, and where am I?"

"Destino is upstairs in his bedroom. You're downstairs in the study, in the room next to where Queen Butcher has been laid. I'll get you to a proper bedroom soon enough, darling. We were worried to jostle you too much going up the stairs."

Panic wells up in me. "That's too far! I have to be closer to Des. Ronin, help me find him!" I try to sit up, but Healer

Wesley and Ronin both back me down onto the… maybe I'm lying on a couch? I can't tell.

"Easy, easy. You need to rest. Destino isn't going anywhere. You can see him when you're feeling better."

"We're connected! *I'm* his headache. If we're apart, he's never going to get better. You have to take me to him! We can't be separated."

"Darling, you're not making any sense." Ronin postures, his nostrils flaring. "Healer, if something's wrong with her mind, I need to know straightaway. We must fix it."

I don't know how to make him understand, and I can't get up. "I need Des!" I shout, my own volume making me wince. "Help me find him! Des!"

"He shouldn't be bothered right now. When we found him, he was passed out on the floor. I don't know if he's been attacked, or what the extent of his injuries might be. He's resting."

"He won't ever get better unless we're together! I'm coming, Des!" I call through the mansion, though I'm certain he can't hear me.

Ronin shoots the healer a look of frustration, as if me throwing what looks like an irrational tantrum is poor Wesley's fault. "Very well, since you won't calm down, I'll take you to him."

"I'll take her, your majesty."

"I'm perfectly capable."

"If I'm the healer, ye have to let me make these kinds of calls. She may have broken something."

"Can she be moved or not? If she can, I'll do it."

The protective note hits me at just the right angle, and I realize how much I really do love this insufferable man.

"Aye," Healer Wesley sighs. "But I'm watching ye."

"Are you intent on a beheading?" Ronin snips, but to his credit, Healer Wesley takes my care seriously as Ronin lifts me off the couch and carries me through the hallways. Everything hurts, but when I get closer to Des' room, all thoughts of my bumps and bruises are shoved to the back of my mind.

17

BY DESTINO'S SIDE

LILYA

Ronin tries to soothe me, but it's no good until I take in the flaccid form of Des as he flops onto his bed. "Easy, now. Here we are. See? Destino is perfectly whole. Just a headache. I imagine it's far less painful than yours."

"Des, what is it?" Prince Alexavier's voice does funny things to my heart and my stomach. I worry I'll vomit again, but when Ronin lays me beside his great-grandson on the bed, everything in me starts to settle. Prince Alexavier touches Des' forehead and turns to Ronin. "He was writhing in agony just a minute ago. Kept trying to get to the door and go downstairs. Gripping his head. Now he's all limp. Healer Wesley, will you look at him?"

I don't care that they're prying at Des' eyes and asking him questions he's too far gone to answer. I can feel the heat from his body sinking into mine. We both shudder together, and when Des finally speaks, his voice catches with emotion he doesn't hold back. I love that about him. "I had a terrible time trying to get to you. Your head! Oh, blue eyes. How did... I... I'm so sorry I couldn't get to you."

I can't roll onto my side, which feels bruised beyond repair, but Des can, so he curves his body around my supine form while we both shudder with relief. The mournful sound that comes from me might've embarrassed me on other days, but I'm too far gone to care about things like decorum right now. "I'm sorry I was taken away from you! I'm here now, Des. We're together."

"My arm," he says as he lightly squeezes my bicep. "I can feel my right arm again. It's not perfectly functional, but I can move it."

Everything in me feels relief just being near him. To know his arm isn't permanently damaged? My body, sore as it is, feels like it's flying. "That's good, Des. How is the rest of you?"

Ronin and Healer Wesley step toward the other side of the room to talk quietly. I want to ask them what they're discussing, but I truly can't handle one more thing.

Des burrows his nose in my cheek as a solitary tear trickles down the side of my face. He kisses the spot, like my pain is a secret only we can share. "Agony. It's been so many hours of torment. I can finally think, now that the pain is gone. You're here. You're here." Des repeats it like a mantra over and over. "I need you. Just a little taste. I need blood, but I can't bring myself to leave your side. Just the stuff you've already shed. I won't bite you."

My fingers lift to lay lifelessly against his cheek. "Whatever you need. I'm just glad you're going to be okay."

He turns my chin up so he can get a good gander at my headwound. I don't particularly like the feeling of his tongue lapping at my temple, but I suppose I have to get cleaned up somehow. He holds me tenderly with his weakened arms, his body engulfing mine in a sensual hug while he licks the side of my face from jaw to forehead. *How bloody am I?*

When a moan of pleasure leaks from his lips, Ronin shouts out a warning and runs to us, gently pulling me away from Des toward the far edge of the bed.

Des reaches for me with desperate arms. "You don't understand! I need more blood!"

"You'll get sick if you drink directly from a fae! She's on Green Lightning, Destino. How delirious are you?" Ronin holds my torso to his chest and kisses my forehead so sweetly, I nearly burst into tears. "He's confused, darling. I won't let anyone hurt you."

What a promise that is. I can barely process the grand nature of his pledge, so I tuck it in my heart and savor the sweetness I didn't know I desperately needed to hear.

My fingers find Ronin's shirt, the loose ends of his tie fluttering against my cheek. "Des doesn't hurt me. He needs me." My hand migrates to his bicep, grateful Ronin lets me hold onto him whenever I wish. "I'm not on Green Lightning. It's okay. We've done this before."

"You, what?" Ronin shouts, looking down on me with horror. "Oh, children, what have you done?" Ronin lays me back down so he can untuck his shirt. He looks a bit comical when he's disheveled. He feels around on the small of his back and produces a small disc like the one Des occasionally carries. "Here, take this. It'll tide you over so you can stop drinking from her. No wonder you were in such pain. It's been so long since I've seen a vampire daft enough to drink directly from a fae; I didn't recognize the symptoms. Of course. Healer Welsey, I need a dose of Green Lightning for my princess." He places the disc on Des' tongue and then steps back, his head resting in his hand. "Oh, the mess you two have made for each other. Do you understand what you've done?"

I don't care about any of it. "Des was starving to death, Ronin. I couldn't care less what society thinks. And I missed my Green Lightning dose because I was trapped in the Stone Graveyard by General Klein, and then had to leave fae territory before I could get a booster."

"You didn't have to leave Faveda!" Prince Alexavier shouts from somewhere behind me. I can't see him, and I don't want to. It's too painful.

"Go away," I tell my fae husband. "I'll take care of Des. And when someone tells me where Salem's gone, I'll look after him, too. Where is he?" I ask Ronin.

Healer Wesley dabs at my forehead with a wet rag again, no doubt determined to remove all traces of blood so Des has nothing to treat himself to. "Salem, Justice and Vera are recovering downstairs. They're still passed out. As soon as you're settled, I'll go check on them. Salem and Justice are bloody, though not as bad off as you are. Vera will recover just fine. Looks like the flowers you conjured up made her pass out. Whoever attacked you all must've put the flowers there so they could escape. But we'll find them, your majesty."

Ice zips through my veins. "No! No, you can't leave her with them! She's the one!"

"Who?"

"*I* made the purple petals!" I confess, muscling through my horror of admitting that I hurt people with my magic. "I made them all pass out so she didn't escape. So she didn't kill us."

"Who?"

"Vera! She took a shovel to my head. She wanted to kill me. I'm pretty sure she was planning on killing Justice and Salem; she attacked them because they saw her go after me. You have to get her away from them! She's dangerous!"

"I'll go," Prince Alexavier offers, running out of the room without need for further explanation.

Ronin puts two fingers to the bridge of his nose. "Darling, what are you on about? That makes no sense. You can't do magic. You told me as much. You hit your head very hard, and the details are getting scrambled." Ronin sits on my bedside, holding my hand like the very best kind of friend. "You saw Vera down there and must've gotten confused. Now think hard; who else was there who could've produced those flowers? Is there another fae in Jacoba?"

"No! I know what happened, and it'll happen all over

again if you don't lock Vera up right now. Come on, Des. We have to help Salem and Justice."

Des is already on his feet, but he sways as his eyes roll back, too lightheaded to take a step. He plops back down on the mattress with a groan, his head in his hands. "Too soon. Ronin, send guards to help Alex. If Lily's wrong, so bloody what. We'll get to the bottom of it. But until then, keep them separate. Don't let Vera go until we know the truth."

Ronin tugs a wrinkle out of my pillowcase. "I highly doubt the woman who's looked after the princes of Jacoba throughout their entire lives would attack them. It makes no sense."

I grip Ronin's hand but I'm so weak, I'm not sure it has the desired effect. "It's her. When Salem and Justice come to, they'll tell you the same. She's not to be alone with them." The regal command sounds odd on my tongue, but I own the words all the same. "Vera's not to leave this house. A guard, Ronin. Lots of them. Promise me."

The hesitation in his eyes worries me, but eventually, Ronin nods, touching Des' forehead with what can only be described as paternal concern. "Alright. I suppose keeping her in a separate room does no one any harm."

A wave of exhaustion sweeps through me. "Promise me."

Ronin sighs. "I just did, darling. Ho, no. You're not to close your eyes." He lightly slaps my cheek, and I fight to keep from slugging him. "You've got a concussion."

"Screw you," I murmur, which draws a gasp from

Healer Welsey. I'm sure he's shocked that anyone would dare talk so disrespectfully to a monarch.

Ronin chuckles, pulling my upper half into his arms. "Get good and uncomfortable. I'm going to hold you sitting upright until this healer of yours deems the worst to be behind you. We can have lots of long chats while we pass the time. How about we start with how you managed to access fae magic you told me you didn't have?"

I can't hide my grimace. "I think I prefer the coma."

"Tricky fae, indeed. Tell me." The serious note comes out like a command.

"No." At his raised eyebrows, I add, "You'll leave. When Prince Alexavier heard the whole story, he left me. I love you too much. I can't risk it." And I know that I truly can't. I need a parent not to hate me, to stay with me while the world shifts and breaks on its journey to rebuilding. I need a parent not to try and murder me, and I've seen Ronin kill his own flesh and blood over a lot less.

"Prince Alexavier left you? Alexavier ended your marriage?"

It's too many details and my brain still feels fuzzy, so Des takes the reins as he gathers his bearings, sitting on the other side of the bed with his back against the oak headboard. "Alex is still married to her, but in name only. The plan is moving forward, but Alex is stepping back."

Ronin's jaw ticks. "I see. This must be quite the secret. Very well, hold onto it as tight as you wish. But I will pry it from your hands sooner or later."

My fingers reach up to trace the skin under his eyes.

"You fainted. I heard you say that when you were rescuing me. Did the petals make you pass out?"

Ronin's neck shrinks. "Just for a moment. The room wasn't properly ventilated, but Alexavier pulled me to safety before I fell completely to ruin."

I chew on my lower lip. "I did that to you. I didn't mean to hurt you. Did you bump anything?"

"Only my pride," he assures me, offering a gracious smile that's meant to cover over my sins.

"I'm sorry," I whisper.

He kisses my forehead, and I love him. I hurt a man I truly care for. I wasn't sure I could feel worse than I already do, but that seals it.

Prince Alexavier's voice reaches us before he enters the room. My heart soars at the sound and then sinks further into the muck. "Vera's gone! Salem's waking up, and his story matches my wife's. Vera attacked them."

I fight the urge to yell "I told you so!" Of course this happened. Of course Vera escaped. I didn't plan for this. I can't protect my family if she's roaming about in the shadows.

"Benny," Ronin says to Prince Alexavier once he comes through the doorway. "Healer Welsey, tell Benny to secure the mansion. The shifter guards protect the Jacoba throne, sure, but not the Drexdenberg crown. Benny is downstairs. He needs to know all of this."

"Aye, your majesty."

No sooner does Healer Wesley disappear into the hallway than Des moves to his feet, bracing himself on the wall. "Salem needs to tell the guards to lock the mansion down. No one comes in or out."

Prince Alexavier holds up his hands. "Salem's already sent for his captains. They've been instructed to find Vera and bring her in." Prince Alexavier's eyes rest on me for the briefest of moments. I'm warm for a second, and then infinitely colder. "They'll find her, Lily-girl."

"Lilya," I correct him. And then I turn to bury my cheek in Ronin's chest. I can deal with Vera. I can deal with Salem having a secret girlfriend. But Prince Alexavier? I'm not sure I'll ever be ready to be near him.

Ronin doesn't know everything, but he knows enough for his arms to tighten around me, shielding me through my devastation at seeing the fae prince again. Ronin cradles my head against his chest and kisses my filthy hair. "Very good, Son. Make sure the mansion is locked down, and then go sit with Prince Justice. Makes sure he's safe until he wakes."

Prince Alexavier hesitates, but then leaves as fate takes him away from me once more.

18

TOO LITTLE, TOO LATE
DESTINO

It's been an hour, and still no word from the soldiers that Vera's been found. "There's nothing we can do right now," I assure Lily.

She's lucid finally, but still weak and stumbly. Each time she tries to get out of the bed, Ronin and I back her down. She's stubborn, determined that she'll get down the stairs to check on Justice and Salem. "The guards can't protect them like I can!" she argues. It's not pride that sharpens her tone but desperation.

"Salem is on his feet," I assure her. "He doesn't need shielding right now. He's doing what he can to protect *you*. And Healer Wesley is seeing to Justice. They've got guards posted outside his room. He'll be alright, blue eyes."

"Don't call me that when I'm about to fight you!"

My eyes widen at her moxie. I don't know why I always underestimate the power it holds. "Is that so? You're going to fight me because I want to keep my family safe just as much as you do? You cannot help anyone until you can walk in a straight line!"

She grumbles at me so sharply that, for a second, it sounds like a feral growl. I contemplate flicking her nose just to really set her off, but I tuck away my childish behavior and do my best to think like a husband. Like a friend. Like a king. "Vera will be caught and punished. Justice, Salem and you will heal, thank the clouds." I watch her shoulders lower, and I hope I'm getting through to her. "Everything is in motion. Best we stay here while the soldiers do what they've been trained to."

Of course, that's the precise moment when Alex enters the room, tightening her up all over again. "Ronin, my mother is hoping to have a word with you in the study."

Ronin sighs. "I cannot be bothered with anything until my children are on their feet."

Now I'm his child? It's a stark difference, going from the great-grandson he didn't loathe, but always made clear I didn't have what it took, to now I'm his child, the one he'll be handing his crown to. Part of me is grateful he finally sees me, and the other part is indignant that for so many years, he didn't see me at all.

Alex shoves his hands in his pockets. "Mother doesn't travel to Jacoba very often, so all of this drama is a little much for her. I posted extra guards outside the study where she's sequestered herself, but she's anxious to get the plans for peace in place so she can go back home."

Alex is wearing the standard white pants and matching shirt. The fae prefer pure garments, spotless and devoid of all the colorful things in the world. I would think the blood stain on his breast would bother him enough to change his shirt, but Alex is more ours than he is theirs. That's always been true, but it hasn't felt like it since our rift. He used to go home from our adventures covered in dust, mud and grass stains. Now he's clean, all but for the blood streak over his heart. It's like he's wearing Lily's blood as a statement that she belongs close to him, even though he's pushed her away. I highly doubt Alex understands himself why he does the things he does, so I don't get terribly bent out of shape when I don't understand him at all.

Ronin rolls his eyes and huffs. "This whole journey here was supposed to be the three current heads of the territories talking about the years to come with the future rulers so we can all get on the same page. We can't exactly do that if one of the heads is still out of commission, and you've got a concussion."

Lily holds her head as if it's too heavy for her neck to support. She should be lying down, but the most I can accomplish is getting her to sit on the bed, which is growing increasingly difficult the more determined she is to get to Salem.

I fluff her pillow, but not even that tempts her to lie down. "Queen Kloe is here? I thought Daddy Fairbucks did most of the actual rulemaking."

Alex takes a step toward her, but I hold out my hand in

warning. Normally I wouldn't keep Alex from a woman he desires, but he's mucked up too much to be near her when she's this injured and turned around. He didn't want her when she was healthy, so he cannot have her when she's taken ill.

Alex respects my boundary and shoves his hands back into his pockets. "Father does because that's who he is, but Mother has just as much power; she just never believes in herself enough to access a drop of it. When the letter arrived from Lily, requesting the rulers to meet to discuss how to end the wars between our territories, she hid your letter from Father and came here in secret. Whatever treaty you want signed, she can sign on behalf of Faveda, and it will hold."

Lily bites down on her lower lip, no doubt processing the same shock I am. I gape at Alex. "Your mum stood up to old Fairbucks, did she? Never thought I'd see the day."

Alex's head bobs. "She stood up to me, too. Made me see what a selfish baby I've been. Lily, I..."

"Lilya," she corrects him, as she has every right to do.

Alex takes her reproach in stride, his mouth snapping shut as he bows his head. "Yes, my queen."

Good. Don't go trying to undo everything malicious you've done with a simple apology. She deserves a good grovel, and she should be well enough to appreciate it.

"I'll go down and talk with her," Lily offers. "This whole thing was my idea. She did a brave thing by coming and standing against King Fairbucks. I don't want her courage to crack by making her wait too long in a place she's clearly scared to be."

Ronin crouches down to kneel in Lily's eyeline before I can do more than shake my head. "No, you won't go anywhere. If this Vera person is bent on coming after you, I want you somewhere safe while your concussion passes. Would you like me to go talk with Queen Kloe?"

Lily reaches out and grips his collar, and then winds her hand behind his neck. "The room keeps tilting," she whispers. I hate that she tells Ronin her secrets. I'm standing right here. I know she's got a fair amount of pride in her, but eventually she'll need to lean on me. I promise myself I'll be patient while we both learn this very important lesson.

"Deep breaths," he instructs her, thumbing her cheek before he kisses it. "You'll stay in this room with Alexavier and Destino. You'll stay in this bed until I tell you otherwise. You'll let Salem protect his household, yes?" He kisses her other cheek, and the urge to slug him tightens my fist. "And you'll let me tend to the smaller duties, which is what a good ruler would do. You're delegating this task to me, which is very wise of you."

Her lower lip puckers. "I hate when you do that—compliment me while doing something I don't like."

The corner of Ronin's mouth lifts. Only Lily can make him smile when things are this tense. "Then I shall do it twice as much."

My chest puffs when Ronin passes by me and claps my shoulder twice. He trusts me, which is something I never would've thought possible a year ago. "Whatever you talk about with Queen Kloe, nothing happens without Lily and us involved," I warn him.

"Good man," he says, granting me a sliver of a smile that's laced with a glint of respect I feel I've finally earned.

19

SECRETS AND GRUDGES

DESTINO

The moment the door closes, Alex and I lock eyes until I give him a small nod, accepting that he's allowed to be here. To be sure, I hate that Alex is in the room, not because I want him out of the picture, but because now Lily's even more anxious. I want to leave the two of them so they can duke it out, but no way am I letting her out of my sight so soon after she was attacked, especially not with her assailant still looming about out there. And Alex hasn't exactly earned the right to look after her while she's vulnerable.

"I hate that it was Vera," I confess. I'm not certain which one of them I'm talking to. I'm not sure it matters. "I always thought her jokes about me being rubbish were funny. I mean, I guess I knew they weren't always jokes, but maybe that's what I told myself they were. I can't believe she attacked her own boys. She practically raised them."

Lily leans forward, cradling her head in her hands while she rests her elbows on her knees. "This is just the start. This is what uniting the territories is going to bring out. We might think we're doing the right thing, but Justice got hurt because of our plan." She looks defeated, which is a hefty shift from the fight I witnessed in her eyes moments ago. "A lot more people are going to splinter apart before they come together. The peace we're working toward? We might not see it in our lifetimes." Her eyes flick to me. "Well, you will."

Everything in me tightens. I try not to think about things like that, about a future without the guys, without Lily. The hazards of being immortal are that you end up saying goodbye to people you don't have the strength to leave. "Don't talk like that. I'm not ready for it."

"Like what?"

The other vampires don't have the same dread because they don't care about people outside our race. They don't understand how painful it is to love as I do.

Alex jumps in and saves me from having to spell out the thing we never discuss. "We don't talk about the fact that we'll all age and die but Des won't. It scares him. Without us, he'll have Ronin and that's all. He'll have the people and duty, but no laughter."

Any traces of hardness on her features melts as her gaze lands on me. I stare up at the ceiling, not willing to be part of this conversation. I like my denial. It serves me well. Denial will be my very best friend and stay with me long after they've all...

"Des without laughter? I cannot picture it," she muses. When she stands on wobbly legs to cross the room in my direction, I open my mouth to scold her, to tell her to sit back down.

Two steps in, her knees go out. I move to catch her, but Alex is closer, and manages to get his arms around our wife before her knees slam into the stone. "Taking up running, are you?" he teases.

It's too soon for jokes, and I wince at her glare once her eyes stop swimming from the sudden motion. "Do not catch me when I fall," she snaps. There's pure venom in her tone, and I won't rob her of it.

Alex swallows his smile and helps her to the bed. "You're right to be mad at me." His hands find their way into his pockets again as he leans against the wall beside my bed. His body language says he's at ease, but I see the tightness in his arms and shoulders. I note the bags under his eyes. "I shouldn't have left you like that. I shouldn't have left at all."

"But you did, so go. Your father's back in Faveda. That's where you belong. Des can make sure I don't trip over my own two feet."

"You're my wife," Alex says, but the words that sound like a plea on his lips hit the air and turn hollow by the time they reach Lily.

Her eyes pierce him through, and when she responds, she chooses her words slowly. "I'm your nothing. I'd just been attacked by a monster, and then my own father. Salem and I barely survived the Stone Graveyard. Des was inches from death, and you were worried about details. So go back to your father and fuss about the details."

Alex is quiet for a beat, letting her anger sizzle between them. "I was upset. You lied to me, Lily-girl. You told me you couldn't perform magic at all. Imagine my surprise when you're the most gifted poison-maker I've ever come across. On top of which, you murdered a whole slew of children and got away with it."

Brilliant apology, dumbass.

"Lilya," she corrects him, her hand on her forehead. "And if you think I got away with anything, you haven't been paying attention. Maybe the label didn't get slapped on me, but I got a death sentence from my own father. When I managed my way out of that, I got a life sentence in Neutral Territory—something not even adult mass-murders are treated to because the fae think that's too cruel. Tell me how I didn't pay for my crimes! Tell me now that I got off easy."

I can't listen to her talk like this about herself. "It was a mistake, Lily! If this was any other child, you wouldn't call them a murderer. You would call them a child who needs help. You were eight years old when you accidentally poisoned your classmates!" I turn to Alex. "And if you think a person is going to be forthcoming about her mistakes when they were punished harsher than an adult would be as an eight-year old, you are more privileged and spoiled than anyone I know. You're the first fae she'd seen in over a decade! Do you think she's going to risk telling you the thing her own father tried to have her killed for?

You get loads of chances in life because of who your parents are and what your title is. She made one mistake. One." I shake my head at him. "And then she made a second mistake by not telling you about it, and you did the same thing her father did when she stepped out of line. You cut her out and threw her away."

"Take that back." Alex seethes, his hands coming out of his pockets to ball into fists. "I'm nothing like General Klein."

I should keep my mouth shut and let them duke it out, but it feels too good to tell the truth. I can't reel myself back now. "Go back to your family, General Alexavier. Leave your wife to me."

Yeah, that was one too far. I don't even brace myself when Alex lunges at me and knocks me backwards. Neither of us really wants to hurt each other, so we end up in a series of pins, holds and escapes, pins, holds and escapes. My right arm isn't exactly one-hundred-percent, but it moves enough so I get in a few licks. We don't stop for Lily's cries of frustration. I'm livid with him for leaving Lily. For leaving me when I was barely alive. For leaving Salem to look after her without backup while he muddled through the new world of being mated. My right arm is frustrating me, so I use my left to punch his kidney.

It's not until a firm hand grips my ear and tugs that I give up on our fight. Our breaths come out in pants and murmured threats as none other than Ronin intervenes. "I thought you were downstairs with the others." I shake him off me and rub my smarting ear.

"There's nothing to be decided upon until Justice awakes. I knew the truth wouldn't come to me directly, so I've been waiting in the hallway so I could have myself a little listen," Ronin admits, locking eyes with Lily. "It was going to take you years to tell me your secret, so I cheated and found a simpler way. Be as livid as you like, only know that you don't have to hide from me anymore."

Her cheeks are pink as she splutters. "You... That's not... You misunderstood everything you think you heard!"

Ronin chuckles as he releases Alex with a shove toward the opposite wall. "I'm sure I did. I'm also sure I understand enough now to know I don't care. If anything, you're more my daughter than ever before. No doubt your birth father didn't like that he saw himself in you, what with how bloody his hands are. But I rather like the sight of myself in you. There will be no more hiding." Then he turns to me. "And what's this about you almost dying?"

Alex brushes the floor dirt off his clothes, and I almost smile because he looks more like himself this way, stained and scowling, blond hair askew. He points his finger at Lily. "I'm drawing you a bath because you're covered in dried blood and dirt. I screwed up, sure, but despite how long you want to send me to the doghouse, I'm not leaving your side again. We'll work this out. I don't care how long it takes."

She turns up her nose at him. "There's nothing to work out. I can't undo what I did. I can't apologize for the rest of my life to someone who has no clue what I've been through."

Alex's voice rises and he starts talking with his hands. "I can't discuss this with you when you look as if you've been freshly killed! Maybe I was upset before, but whatever reasons I thought were important enough to leave you over seemed stupid the moment I reached my palace without you. You are my home, the three of you." His eyes flick to Ronin. "Not you, obviously. Salem. Des can wrestle me to the ground to keep me in line, Salem can punch me, and Lily, you can push me away, but I'm still here." He points to the floor between them. "You screwed up by not telling me the truth before we married. Spin it however you want but we know each other. I deserve all the information when I'm signing a legally-binding document. But I screwed up by leaving instead of staying by your side and battling this out. I shouldn't have left you. You fight for what matters, and I didn't fight for you. For that, I'm truly sorry."

Alex's voice breaks on the last sentence. His eyes mist over, so I go still, unsure what to make of the tenor in the room.

Lily's anger cracks, and finally she lets him peek into her heartbreak. "You were taken from me when we were kids. I didn't think anything could feel worse than that. But when you left on your own, after knowing my most terrible parts, *that* was worse. That's the gut-punch I can't come back from."

"I shouldn't have left you," Alex says again, his eyes pleading with her to understand.

"You don't know a thing about survival! You don't know what it is to be the only fae around for years! You threw me away because I wasn't shiny enough. You're just like every other fae!"

"I shouldn't have left you." Then Alex turns on his heels and moves into the washroom. I hear water splashing in the tub and fight the urge to go comfort Lily. She doesn't need to come down from her anger. She doesn't need me to mold her fury into a peaceful ending. Alex deserves every ounce of it aimed straight at his chest.

We haven't bathed in over a week. None of us. The shifters don't have water to spare for vanity or hygiene.

There's silence for too many minutes. Ronin starts to speak, but Lily holds up her hand with a firm, "Don't," so he backs down.

When Alex comes out of the washroom, his chin is lowered like an animal who knows he's done wrong. "Your bath is ready. I would help you, but I'm guessing you don't want that."

"You belong where you put yourself, which is with your father, not with me. You're welcome to help *him* in the bath as much as you'd like."

Alex meets my eyes with agony shining through. "You'll need to help her, Des. She still can't walk without falling. It won't do us any good if she drowns in two feet of water."

As angry as I want to be, I know his punishment right now is worse than anything I could dole out. Being separated from the woman your insides are screaming to be near is excruciating.

I cross the room and gather him up in a hug meant to hold us together, even when we've been torn apart by too much life. He slumps in my arms so much that his head rests on my shoulder. "I'm sorry, Brother. I left you when you were barely alive. Lily gave you back to us, and I…"

"I know. You were bloody stupid, but I love you anyway."

He manages a chuckle through what I'm certain are the beginnings of tears forming. "I love you, Des."

I slap him twice on the back. "I'll watch her. Why don't you see what help Salem needs?"

Alex pulls away with a nod and opens the door for Ronin, who's also being shooed out.

The moment they're gone, I close my eyes and lean against the door, grateful for the quiet that falls around us like promises of peace. When I open my eyes a few beats later, Lily's staring at me. "I'm glad it's you," she says simply. "That's it's just you. No one else."

I know exactly how she feels. "You're the only person I want to see right now, too. It's been a long one, yeah?"

Her chest expands and contracts violently just once, but it's enough to let me know she's on the brink of breaking down.

Finally.

My alone time with Lily seems to always come in the middle of too much turmoil for either of us to actually enjoy the moment. But now, as she takes my hand and I lead her into the bathroom, she lets me undress her with slow fingers and gentle kisses meant to heal the broken parts of us both. When the last of Lily's clothes fall to the floor, the sight of her standing before me forces the rest of the world's troubles to fade into the background.

She's not embarrassed. She's not terribly unsteady as she leans against the door.

She's mine. Entirely and completely mine, if only for this moment.

I can't not kiss her. I know she's concussed. I know I've barely got partial use of my right arm back. I know all the reasons we should wait yet again for the thing I crave above all else. When my lips find hers, my left arm acquaints itself with the slope of her side. My fingers trill over her hip, teasing the chilled skin that warms for me.

"Des, is it wrong to want you right now? I know things are all messed up out there, but in here, I just want…"

"Then you shall have me, any way you like. Whatever pleases my queen." I love the way she blushes whenever anyone reminds her of her future title. I get to enjoy the full scope of her skin as it colors and fades in places that are entirely new to me. It's not enough to admire them; I need to touch each inch that calls out to me. I've never seen a naked fae woman before, and I'm completely mesmerized. "Which parts of you are hurt from the attack?" I ask quietly between kisses. If we're going to do this, I don't want to injure her further.

"My head and my ribs on this side," she admits. "But this is what I want. Please, Des. We've been married for months. I don't think I can wait another second for the honeymoon. There's too much going on outside that door. Make me forget. Make me forget it all."

It's a true effort not to hurriedly rip my clothes off, but take my time seducing her, kissing every inch she offers me until her knees begin to quake. "I've wanted this for so long." I kiss her over and over, capturing each gasp between my teeth as my hands do as she pleases, roaming where she needs.

Finally, my clothes join hers. The second I carry her to the water and lower us in, there's only her, me, and the sultry sounds the water makes as it laps against our bare skin while we make good use of our privacy.

20

FIRST HUSBAND, AND SECOND

LILYA

I love everything about Des, down to the way he dries me off from head to toe when we're finally clean. I still have to lean on him, but my dizzy moments are growing fewer and farther between. We don't bother with clothes for the longest time, making this the best part of my stay in Jacoba, for certain. Des' hands on me tease and stroke, making my breath catch over and over again. The wall is like ice against my spine when he presses my shoulders against it. He makes sure my arm is always looped around his neck, holding him close so every part of us is touching. When my knees start to give out, he holds me in place, kissing me slower now, with his hand kneading my butt to keep me from falling.

"Did I hurt you?" he asks, his eyes skimming down over my form.

"Only a little," I admit. "I'm glad it was you."

"I'm your first husband, after all. And you'll always be my only wife."

I kiss him because his lips are addictive. Everything about Des makes me crave him all over again. Though I'm still a little sore, every part of me is ready for more.

"Tell me this is the best you've ever had," Des breathes.

"You're the only I've ever had, so it's not a totally fair statement."

He sniggers airily as he kisses me. "I know I won't always be your only, but for now, I'm on cloud nine."

My heart sinks and our kisses slow. "You will be. Salem has a girlfriend. I can't do this with him when there's someone else out there he already belongs to. I don't care if we're mated. It's wrong to do that to another woman. And Alexavier will leave again. It's just you and me."

Des shakes his head, thumbing the swell of my breast just to watch me arch for him. "As much as part of me would love nothing more than exactly that, it's not going to settle that way. I told you, I would know if Salem had a girlfriend. He doesn't. And eventually, you and Alex will find a path through this. You love him. You love all three of us deviants."

I tell Des the truth because he's the only one I trust with all of it. "I do. I love all three of you so badly, it hurts. I don't want to feel this much. It's hard to be separate from them."

Des is a good sport. He kisses my nose and gives me the best smile I've seen all night. "Then let's go see what they're up to." At my protest, Des shakes his head. "Like it or not, we have to go to this meeting. The powers that be and the powers that *will* be need to find a way to work together. Let's go get dressed, and we'll talk to Salem about this other woman. You'll see it's no one. She doesn't exist. Straighten it all out before the meeting, so you've got a clear head."

"I can't imagine any woman having a clear head when a naked vampire prince is kissing her."

The corner of his mouth drags upward. "Then I should probably put some clothes on." He pauses before letting go of me, his roguish grin doing crazy things to every inch of me that's pressed up against him. "Tell me I'm your king."

I kiss him because I can. Because it's good. Because he's mine. "You're my king. Tell me I'm your lily."

"My very own flower with a crown." His tongue flicks my earlobe before he reaches around and opens the door, letting us into the bedroom.

"Ah!" I squeak and then hop back into the bathroom while Des shuts the door with him on the other side. My ribs instantly protest the sudden movement, so I bend over, holding my side. "You were supposed to go downstairs!" I shout at the closed door.

Prince Alexavier's voice is pinched through the barrier. "I told you I shouldn't have left, so I didn't leave. I'm not going to sit at a meeting you're not there to weigh in on. It's all of us or none of us." Then there's a muffled bit I can't hear, followed by, "Would you put some pants on, Des? Stop strutting around, all cocky."

I tuck the towel around my frame and do my best not

to display my embarrassment as I open the door again and stride out, catching a glimpse of Des sliding on his boxer briefs. The room doesn't tilt anymore, but Prince Alexavier fixes his hand to my elbow to make sure I don't stumble. I don't have it in me to jerk away from him, mainly because I'm not completely certain the room won't slant again at any given second.

"You're bracing yourself. What hurts?" Prince Alexavier's hand flutters over my back and lands on my hip. The touch is so protective and gentle, I nearly lean into it.

My jaw tightens. "You're going to leave. Just get it over with. You being here doesn't make any sense." This is the last thing I want to talk about right now, but it comes out of me without a filter. "It'll be more painful if you pretend to want to be with me, and then leave again."

Prince Alexavier stops our path toward the bed. He turns my body slowly and holds me like he knows how, which is the best and worst thing a man can do after he's left you. "I'm not leaving."

I wasn't expecting him to still be here. I was purposefully harsher with him than I wanted to be because he was supposed to run away when things got difficult. "I can't afford to trust in something that's going to disappear."

Prince Alexavier kisses my forehead. "If I was going to leave, it would've been when I had to listen to you lose your virginity to my best friend on the other side of that wall. If I was going to leave, it would've been when all of this grew to be bigger than I could handle. Let me stay, Lily-girl."

When his arms tighten around my waist, there's no lie in them. But to be safe, I press my ring to his chest. "Why are you here?" It's not a challenge so much as a search for the truth. I need to hear nothing but total honesty, even if it hurts.

Prince Alexavier looks deep into my eyes, his stomach flush to mine. "I'm here because I love you. And I'm not leaving until you understand exactly that. All those years that were stolen from us weren't our fault. But this small stretch was agony because *I'm* the one who broke it. I wasted too many days staying away from you when that was never meant to be our destiny." My ring sinks deeper, my hand warm with a melting chocolate sensation that spreads over his chest. It's the same feeling I get when Des promises me all the ways we'll always have each other. There's not a trace of coldness, no hint of a lie. "We're supposed to stay together, even when you're scared of yourself. Even when I'm wrong."

"You're telling me the truth," I confirm aloud.

"I wouldn't have come all this way for a lie." He thumbs the small of my back, and my body hums in that exact spot. "One day—not today, but one day—will you forgive me for forgetting we belong together?"

I study the sincerity in his eyes, the curve of his lips, the lack of laughter in him. It's an effort to loop my arm around his neck, but I take that leap as I grant him a small nod. His entire being exhales aloud when I lean my head on his shoulder and his arms tighten around my hips. "I'm still mad at you," I admit, though that anger is lessened with every inhale I take from the crook of his neck.

"That's okay. I'm mad at me, too. It's not going to heal easy or quick, but so long as you'll give me a chance, I'll make sure it heals." His lips press to my naked shoulder, and goosebumps rip across my flesh, awakening for him. He kisses my neck, stealing rough gasps from me as my knees weaken. "How angry are you right now? So livid that I shouldn't kiss your lips?"

I don't know how to answer that, so I dive into the deep end and kiss him.

It's one step too far, so my knees buckle. My vision swims, and I'm so pissed at Vera for putting me in this predicament that the only thing that comes out of me is a loud curse word as Alexavier struggles to keep me upright.

Des rushes to my other side, and the two of them help me to sit on the edge of the bed.

I groan as I lean forward. "Ugh. That was supposed to be sexier than it went down. This stupid concussion."

"Easy, then. Deep breaths." Des sits beside me and anchors me to him until the room stops spinning. He's dressed in only his underwear, so I get to take as much warmth from his skin as I like. He takes my hand and holds it atop his bare thigh, covering my chilly fingers with his because that's how much Des loves me. "Close your blue eyes and give yourself a moment to catch up. Alex will still be just as dashing then, yeah?"

It takes me more than a minute to open my eyes, and when I do, I'm treated to the sight of Alexavier kneeling before me, dirtying his white outfit just to make a statement. Though my ribs still ache, my head is clearing, which is half the battle. "Sorry about that."

Alexavier purses his lips at my apology, but doesn't say anything. Instead he stands, tilting my chin up so he can kiss me without fear of me falling to the floor.

Our lips move slowly, letting the seduction feel like friendship for as long as it needs to. It's us, and for all the confusion and hurt I'm still holding on to, being us is exactly what I want right now.

Though neither of us are going to kick Des out, he's polite enough to give us our reunion. He slides on his pants and tugs a shirt over his head. "I think I'll pop downstairs and have a look around. See if Vera's hiding in any abandoned rooms, broom closets or dust bins."

Alexavier freezes at my gasp and pulls back to examine my epiphany. I try to stand again, completely killing the mood. "Queen Butcher! Des, that's where she'll be!"

"I was joking," Des admits, holding up his hands. "Lily, there's no way Vera's in the mansion still. She would have fled first thing."

"She doesn't want to escape." As the words come out of me, I'm certain I'm right. "Vera attacked Queen Butcher because she was about to sign a peace treaty with Ronin."

Des' eyebrows shoot upward. "What? When was this?"

"Years ago. Back when Queen Butcher was awake, obviously. Vera poisoned her, but she has to keep giving Queen Butcher regular doses of bella donna because otherwise the queen might wake back up. Vera never had the courage to kill her, but now that Vera's got nothing to lose? She's going to finish the job."

Des shoves on his boots and runs out of the room, while Alexavier helps me find clean-ish clothes, sighing his frustration that the most naked we'll be getting is him watching me dress. He lets me lean on him while we make our way down the halls, toward where I'm certain Vera will return.

21

BROTHER JUSTICE

LILYA

I feel more myself, now that I'm in my jeans and navy long-sleeved t-shirt with my holster strapped around my thigh. Maybe I don't look shifter or vampire or even fae like this, but I can think clearer, understanding the next step I have to take. Queen Butcher's room was promptly searched upon my accusation, but Vera was nowhere in sight.

That doesn't bother me one bit. I can wait. There aren't just guards posted at each exit, but one of us is there as well. While Salem trusts his guards, he also trusted Vera, so I put my foot down that we're hedging our bets. There are soldiers scouring the area for her, but so far, no one's seen a hair on her gray head.

They told me to wait in Des' bedroom so I'm safe, but I'm unused to the high premium they place on my life. I tried. I really did. I stayed for ten minutes before I got the itch to move. I'm not accustomed to waiting around while someone I love might be in danger. In this case, it's many someones, plus Salem's mother, who deserves more protection than guards at the exits.

I do what I can to move quietly. I don't want another lecture from Ronin about what it means to be a ruler. Letting other people do the heavy lifting when there's work to be done doesn't feel like ruling to me. It feels like being a sitting duck while the world burns around me. I don't have much tolerance for that. Ronin's anxious to get Des and me to sit down with him for some big talk, but there are more important things at hand. Des is positioned near the east exit, which is about halfway between the room I'm supposed to be in upstairs, and Queen Butcher's resting room. My footsteps are light and soundless as I move down hallways, holding my breath and leaning on walls when I get dizzy. I nearly collapse twice, but manage to let myself into her room with a giant gust of relief.

"Ah!" I shout, breaking my silence when giant hands fly towards me, and a body pins me to the wall in the dark. Judging by the bulk that's squishing the air from my lungs and jolting my aching ribs, it's definitely not Vera.

"Lily? What are ye doing here?" Justice's breath is hot in my face.

"Getting mauled by a prince who's supposed to be on bedrest, apparently."

Justice releases me and brushes his hands down my sides, straightening my shirt with an apologetic dip to his head that I can only just make out in the dark. His voice lowers to a terse whisper. "You're supposed to be upstairs, wee lass."

"You're supposed to be resting. You were attacked and then you passed out, if you recall."

"Aye, well, when Destino told me about your theory about where Vera's most likely to be, I decided to make my way over here. Seemed like as good a place as any to recover."

"What's her animal? I'm on edge because I'm not sure what kind of attack I'm in for if she shifts."

"Vera's a harmless calico cat. Nothing like the lebnest monster."

"The what?"

Justice waves his hand. "Mostly a myth. A huge, scaly olive-tinted monster tha breathes fire. I don't think it exists, but a few in Jacoba swear they've seen it in action. The most Vera will do is give ye a kitten's scratch."

"Whew. That's a relief. Yikes on the lebnest monster, though."

He scratches the back of his head. "Destino was tight-lipped about how exactly we escaped the storm cellar. Said ye know more about tha than anyone else, so I should ask ye."

Great. Part of me wants to tell Justice to shove off and just be grateful he's alive. Looking too closely at the details of how it all went down won't do me a lick of good. But, as I'm living under his roof and all, I dig deep for what bravery I have left. The story comes out in choppy whispers as we sink to the stone floor to settle in for the wait, but it comes, hanging between us in the dank air that desperately needs to be vented. I want to open the window so the residual stink of sandalwood and my sins drifts away, reducing to particles of pain that no one can touch.

We sit together on the hard floor, our backs chilled against the stone wall and our knees bunched up on the other side of Queen Butcher's bed. If the door opens, we won't be immediately visible. With each segment of my story, I expect Justice to get up and leave, to cuss me out, to forbid me going near his brother.

But he stays. Justice doesn't leave me, and I'm not completely sure why. As I near the end, confessing how I poisoned Vera, and by default, him and Salem, I prepare myself for his wrath, hugging my knees to my chest as tightly as my bruised ribs will allow.

Instead of all the things I fear, Justice curves his arm around my back when the stone support coaxes a shiver from me. Then he reaches over and tugs a blanket down from the shelf beneath the nightstand. I'm flummoxed when he drapes the heavy brown material over my legs. "What are you doing?"

"You're cold."

"Yeah, but why are you being nice to me?"

Justice chuckles airily, the sound of it staying between us. "What idiot wouldn't be nice to the person who saved them? Vera would've killed me if ye hadn't done what ye did."

My nose scrunches as confusion purses my lips. "I'm

dangerous. I can snap my fingers and produce a poison so deadly, it can burn through flesh."

"Ye may be afraid of yourself, but today I draw breath because of ye. I'll not waste what life you've granted me being afraid of a good thing. Neither should ye."

His words hit me like the slap across the face I needed. Perhaps Fiora was right all those years she told me "magic is what ye make of it." I didn't understand what she meant, or maybe I didn't believe it. But Justice telling me that I'm his good thing gives me faith that maybe I won't be a curse to the world because of who I am.

Justice's arm around my back pulls me closer, until my temple is resting on his meaty shoulder. He trusts in the good parts of me enough to let me near him, so I resolve to always be the thing that saves him, that helps him, that is good for him and his territory. "I won't hurt you," I promise us both.

"I know tha. But I need your word tha ye won't harm Salem or his girlfriend once he comes clean to ye."

All my elation crashes at mention of the thing I've been trying to push out of my mind. "Of course not. I'll do what I have to so the territories are united. This was never about feelings. It was about the people. The future. That hasn't changed."

There's only a beat of silence before Justice's hand moves up and down over my bicep to soothe my palpable ache. "I've seen the way ye look at my brother. It's about feelings, too."

I don't want to need comfort, but the cold is sinking in

deep, penetrating my bones in a way that makes me wonder if I'll ever feel warmth again. "It's okay that we'll have a marriage of necessity. That's how Des and I started out. There are worse things."

Justice sighs heavily. "You're breaking my heart with this, wee bunneh." He goes quiet but his thoughts are loud, creating a sense in me that he's struggling with something.

"What's on your mind?"

With his free hand, he rubs his jaw without looking at me. "I wasn't on the same page as the four of ye with this plan of uniting the territories. I'm not against it; I just didn't think it was possible. I've been coming around on it, and I agree tha this is the way it should be." His chin lowers, and the next words that come out of his mouth are meant just for us. "If Salem won't marry ye, I will."

I can't help the gasp that flings out from my lips. "What?"

He backpedals a little, but holds his ground. "For political reasons, of course. I wouldn't trouble ye for intimate things. I think you're right about the world needing to change, and tha the leaders need to drive the change, rather than always reacting to the chaos. If Salem wants to be with his girlfriend, I wouldn't doom either of ye to suffer tha. You've sacrificed too much already. I'll marry ye, and the territories will have one queen."

My heart thuds in an unnatural rhythm. "You would do that for your territory?"

"No," he admits, rubbing the nape of his neck as he looks anywhere but at me. "I'd do tha for Salem. If he wants to be with another lass but feels this strongly about unity, I can't allow him to sacrifice himself like tha. People think I'm in charge because I'm set as next to rule, but Salem's the one who makes sure the territory stays in line. He's sacrificed enough. I can do this for my brother."

I slump forward, cradling my face in my hands. I don't want the prospect of marrying me to be something a person has to endure to take one for the team. I know that's not the main point, but as honorable as Justice's motivations are, I can't help but wallow in a sea of sadness.

Salem has a girlfriend he's loved for years. I don't understand any of it. Our kiss felt so real. "The way he looked at me..." I begin, but then stop short to keep my lower lip from quivering. Then I clear my throat. "I really thought Salem wanted to be with me, even if it had nothing to do with our master plan. I don't know how I got it all so wrong. Maybe he kissed me so well because of the thrill of cheating on his girlfriend."

We're mated. Justice still doesn't know. I'm not sure how to undo that, or how nature could've gotten this so very wrong. Salem shouldn't have been able to mate with me in the first place, being that we're of two different species. We'll find a way to undo it, I'm sure, and then Salem can kiss his girlfriend with passion that makes her toes curl.

The thought of it breaks my heart.

Justice kisses the top of my head, cradling my creeping depression on his firm shoulder. I can't see him as anything other than a friend or a brother, but I suppose that will have to be enough. It's not about us; it's about territories that need each other. The shifters need water or they will die off. I can marry someone I respect but don't love if it'll get an entire people fresh water.

"It's alright, bunneh. Let's tackle one mountain at a time."

I don't have a plan for any of it, so I nod, letting the silence sit atop the blanket we share.

When the door creaks open however long later, Justice and I still, not daring to breathe as the swish of a skirt sweeps the floor. It's hard to see, but I feel the air stirring in menacing ways. Justice reaches for his knife, but Salem's edict that wrongdoers should be punished and not murdered sits in the front of my mind. Justice needs to stay innocent. He's in charge of an entire territory. He can't have blood on his hands.

My hands are plenty bloody, and ready for the challenge of defending the throne of Jacoba.

22

THE WICKEDNESS IN ME

LILYA

I don't wait for Vera to approach the queen or peer over the bed to glimpse our motionless lumpy shapes in the dark. The blanket slides off my lap as I ready to pounce, but before I make my move, Justice leaps to his feet. He darts around the foot of the bed to throw his body in front of the door, trapping Vera inside with us as he grips his knife.

"Justice!" she shrieks. The moonlight catches on the blade in her hand, and I know she's not here to administer Queen Butcher's regular dose of bella donna. She's come to the end of her rope, and is tying up all loose ends.

It's two steps between her and me before I jump on her back. It's a foolhardy move, but at this point, it's all or nothing. My ribs hurt so badly at the movement; I cry out at the pain I'm causing myself to make sure Justice stays innocent. Despite everything, he loves Vera. I can't let his sweet soul get damaged when mine is already beyond repair and far easier to sacrifice.

"I've got this, Lily!" Justice protests, but it's already done. My palms are sweaty as I cup my hand over Vera's mouth. I don't care about sound leaking out. I care that she gets the full brunt of the petals that bloom from the center of my hand. Her scream as my other arm wraps around her throat traps itself between her lips and my fingers. I could fill her mouth with tiny white flowers. A flash of my childhood tragedy forces its way to the forefront of my mind. I killed them all, and they didn't deserve it. But this woman does. Despite Salem's argument that criminals deserve a fair trial, I don't want to let Salem and Justice endure another minute of this torment.

"I could kill you right now, you know," I seethe, ignoring Justice's shouts as Vera struggles for breath in my chokehold. "But Salem doesn't believe in that. He'll want you to have a fair trial."

She claws at my arm, her fingernails drawing blood on the second swipe.

I'm malicious when I conjure a clump of blue petals in my palm, but maybe I should be magnanimous. Maybe I should leave her unharmed after all she's done, and simply secure her and turn her over to the prison system.

When she finally works out a breathy, "Fae whore!" any doubt steels to resolve.

"I hope you enjoyed your last word. Taste that?" Blue petals are filling her mouth faster than she can spit them out. "Quicker than anything you've got and twice as potent," I tell

Vera as she topples forward onto her knees with a scream I catch in my palm. I fall with her, and she smacks her chin on the stone floor. But I don't call the job done because she's still struggling beneath my weight. My ribs beg me to stop, but my fury over anyone harming Salem holds me in place. Justice is shouting at me, but I don't care enough to make out his words. It's just me and the woman who hurt Salem.

She attacked my mate.

My knees fix to the stone on either side of her, my arm hooked around her neck to keep her head angled where I need it. My hand stays in place over her screams, filling her mouth until the petals spill out.

Her shrieks and desperate twitches don't instill anything in me but a calmness that surpasses everything scared or sad inside my heart. This is what I was born to do, malicious as my magic is. Salem will be safe from Vera now, and I will have protected what's mine. Though he may belong to another woman, in my heart, he is mine to guard, mine to fight for, mine to avenge.

I'm a mix of vengeance and mercy, punishment and grace, not knowing which will win out. I don't know who I want to be, and barely know who I am.

I know who I was—a scared girl who killed her friends, and then an isolated adolescent who feared her own magic. But I'm a woman now, and my magic needs to become what I make of it.

Who do I want to become? What sort of ruler do I want to be?

Purple petals will knock Vera out so the guards can take her away. White petals will rid the world of her once and for all.

Purple or white? Purple or white? Mercy or death?

I finally choose, latching on to the woman I want to become—a ruler who believes in the justice system and can respect its process.

The moment my decision is made, a flurry of petals fill Vera's mouth.

The perfume of the purple fills me with hope that perhaps I'm not the worst version of myself—that there's the possibility of redemption for Vera, and perhaps for me as well.

The purple is my one kindness I offer—to knock her out while the blue flowers eat through her tongue. She inhales the fragrance, and then I shove them in her mouth to keep Justice from breathing them in.

I don't realize how hard my chest is heaving until Vera goes limp beneath me. I close the petals inside of her mouth, knowing full well what a horrible person I am. I'm burning out a person's tongue, and then knocking her out. If Vera wants to poison the world with her venomous words that will only divide us, and attack the throne that gave her such freedoms, she can do so without a functional tongue.

It's not the due process Salem insisted all criminals go through, but it's a compromise from the swift death my fingers are itching to deliver.

I don't want to look at Justice, but in my periphery, I can see the outline of his dropped jaw. "Is she dead?"

"No." I take the hand he offers me and stand to my feet, grimacing as I cradle my side. My ribs are plenty angry I didn't let Justice handle the whole thing with his blade. "Salem frowns on capital punishment. Vera's knocked out for now, and she's going to be different when she wakes up, but she won't hurt your mother ever again."

Justice runs his hand over his face, his eyes wide. "It's me who was supposed to defend my mammy."

"Actually, it's me who's supposed to defend my future mother-in-law, my husband and his brother. Dirty hands don't rule as well as clean ones." I glance down at my hand-iwork. "Besides, you loved Vera. You shouldn't have to be the one to take her down. You don't need that keeping you up at night."

Justice swallows hard as his eyes meet mine in the dark. "Ye did tha for me?"

I nod once. "You're my brother."

Justice is gentle with me as he helps me sit on the floor a fair distance away from Vera. "Ye look like ye might pass out. Stay right here. I'll get the guards. Let them know it's over. Then all we have to do is wait for Mammy to wake up when the poison wears off." He fists the doorknob, but pauses. "I haven't heard her voice in years. Ye... Ye don't know the good you've done for us."

"Get Salem," I say, though there's no one I want to see less in this moment. "I can wake your mom sooner than that, but I'll need his help."

"Aye." The opened door introduces a sliver of light into the room, highlighting emotion ripe in Justice's gray eyes. "I don't know how to thank ye."

I tear my gaze away from his gratitude. I don't feel heroic or happy. I'm weighted with the heaviness that comes when it's clear there are villains in the world we cannot escape. I don't like that I had to take a woman down by force in order to liberate another. I can only hope that when Queen Butcher opens her eyes, she sees the goodness still left in the world, and not the wickedness in me.

23

HANNAH

SALEM

Three days is too long for Lily to be out, but apparently there's nothing I can do for her but wait. I'm torn, wanting to be by her side and never move an inch from her bed, and also getting my mammy acclimated to being upright again. I also need to finish up the project Lily requested. So I spend my days by my mammy's side with Justice, helping her learn to use her muscles again, and explaining to her all she missed while she slept. Then my nights are spent in bed with Lily and the lads. We cuddle close to her, though she can't see or hear us. We're lost pups without her, the whole lot of us. My mate is injured, so my guts feel cobwebby and disgusting as the poison works its way through her.

Alex doesn't leave her side, insisting any contract negotiations are put on hold until Lily is awake to weigh in on them. I like tha he's adamant she has a voice in shaping the future, even though it's not her turn to rule yet.

Alex's mammy looks in on Lily during the day. I've never seen Queen Kloe Fairbucks show interest in anything aside from her martini glass, but I'm grateful for the help. All of us are unifying, whether we realize it or not. We're centered around getting Mammy on her feet again, and seeing Lily through the worst of the illness she took upon herself so my mammy could come back to us faster.

My mate belongs in my bed. My sheets smell like lilies now, and I want to roll around in them for years on end. I can't bring myself to break out of my wolf form at night while Lily's too sick to lift her head, her curls fanned across my pillow. She's perpetually cold, so I keep my fur pressed to her all night long, lifting my head only when Justice pops in to check on her every few hours. Her hair was black after she sucked out Mammy's poison and took it into herself, but it's been slowly changing back to its normal color, adding more beauty to the world than a shifter like me has a right to expect.

"How is she?" my brother asks again. I like tha he cares. She'll be his sister soon. Whatever grudge he's held against her, she's managed to melt with her sweetness. No big surprise there. She saved our mammy and single-handedly brought down our attacker. She deserves more than me, yet somehow, I'm the thing she wants.

"Same," Des answers, while Alex stares vacantly at her form, as if silently willing her to get up.

My whole being stutters when Lily stirs at the sound of Justice's voice, her arm moving over my body in a stretch I've been waiting to witness. I lick her chin and cheeks over and over, coaxing her to come back to me. When her sigh greets me as her arm tightens around my neck, I give a few sharp yowls in case she's considering drifting back to sleep. I can't wait much longer. The suspense of not hearing her voice has been a slow torture.

Alex is at her other side in a flash, his palm tipping to her mouth as he helps me prop her up. A well of water forms and slides between her lips, waking her more fully. Her eyes open as she sags against Alex's chest while Des sits at her feet on the mattress.

"Lexi," she rasps, her eyes closing again. "You didn't leave."

"Never again," Alex vows, and this time, I believe him. It's not the power of his words tha sway me, but the fact tha he hasn't left her side this entire time. "You've been out for three days, and I'm still here."

"Three days? Oh, wow. The bella donna must've been in deep in Queen Butcher. Is she awake? Is she alright?"

Justice answers because I'm too enraptured by the sound of her voice to transform back into a man who can speak to her. I just want to be near her, to watch her lashes open and shut as she tries to regain her bearings. "Mammy's sitting on her own, and even stood for a minute this morning. She's determined to thank ye personally, but wants to be able to get up the stairs on her own first. She's a proud woman," Justice says with a smile. "How are ye feeling?"

She barely works out "A little hungry" before Des is trotting toward the door. "I'll get you something," he offers.

Bastard.

Alex waits until Des is gone before he sprouts a small plant from his palm that blooms berries. "Here you are."

Justice comes further in and sits in the chair by her bedside. "Ye can go back to her," he tells me. "I'll sit with Lily."

I let out a derisive snort at the notion tha anything could part me from my mate now.

"Go on. You've been either with this lot or with Mammy for days. I know all about your little secret affair. So does Lily. Best give her some space now. Besides, Lily will be my wife soon enough. I'll sit with her."

Alex and I both whip our heads in his direction. I'm on two legs in the next breath, standing next to the bed with my fists clenched. "*I'm* to marry her. We already decided."

"Tha's hardly fair to Lily. She knows all about the reason ye disappear for days on end. I can do this duty, Brother. Then ye can go be happy."

"What?"

Alex's nostrils widen. "Salem wants to marry Lily. Did I miss something?"

Lily keeps her eyes from me. "I can marry Justice. It's not a big deal. We talked about it, and it's for the best."

Just like tha, my heart is trampled on by the woman I love most in the world, and by my own brother, which I truly didn't see coming. "What about our kiss? You're my mate! Ye can't marry Justice. Ye can't!"

Justice frowns at me. "What are ye running your gob about? Ye aren't mated. Tha's not possible."

I point to my one blue eye tha's gone largely overlooked. "Ye can't have her. I don't know how it happened, but it did. She's my mate. I'll not let her marry my brother." I shake my head, utterly flummoxed. "Ye really want to marry Justice? Don't ye understand what tha does to me? I can share with Alex and Des, but Justice?" I can't stop shaking my head, lost in a nightmare I'm not sure how I landed myself in.

Justice stands, his mouth falling open at the evidence he can read in my eyes. "It's not possible," he says again.

I don't want to talk to him about it. I don't care tha I look pathetic. I'm a sap for her, and I want the whole world to know it. "I'm in love with ye, Lily. I'm not sure what happened tha you're pulling back now."

She's only just awake, and we're forcing her to talk about all of this far too soon. Her eyes water, but tears don't fall when she shoots me the most agonized look I've ever seen on my mate. "I know you have a girlfriend!"

Of all the things I'm expecting her to say, tha's nowhere on the list. My fists loosen as I take a step back. "What?"

"Justice told me all about it. You should've been straight with me. I'm not someone who takes a guy from another woman. That's not me. And you shouldn't have kissed me like that! Not if you could never be mine." Her sad eyes glance up at Justice. "How do you undo the mate bond?"

A strangled cry breaks out of me, and I stumble back tha she could even consider something so horrible.

"It can't be undone," Justice replies, his eyes on me. "Brother, none of this makes sense. I thought you'd be relieved to go back to Hannah. I offered to marry Lily to let ye off the hook."

"What hook? And how do ye know about Hannah?"

Lily's head whips back and forth between the two of us, hurt and confusion radiating from all corners of the room.

"I overheard ye confessing to Mammy when she was in her coma tha ye were in love with a lass named Hannah. I heard ye say it loads of times when ye didn't think anyone heard. I know ye have a girlfriend you're mad for. I'm trying to help ye!"

I blink at him as the pieces slowly fall into place. "Ye heard me talking about the woman I go to see, aye? Ye heard me tell Mammy how in love I am with this Hannah person?"

Justice nods, and all the color drains from Lily's face. I want to laugh at the absurdity of it all, but I can't until I'm certain Lily understands.

Alex sniggers as I point to Lily. "Tha's Hannah."

Justice's head tilts to the side. "No, tha's Lily. And you've led her on long enough. I heard the way ye talked about Hannah. Ye love her. Ye belong with her."

Lily's voice is small but fills the cracks of my heart, spackling them so they aren't so very broken. "I used to go by Hannah when I lived in Neutral Territory. It was safer that way. Fiora renamed me to protect my identity in case General Klein came looking for me." She tips up her chin in my direction, those wet eyes splintering me into a thousand pieces. "You don't have a girlfriend?"

"Only ye. I meant what I said. I've never had eyes for anyone but ye."

She shakes her head as one tear finally falls. I can't take it. I have to wipe it off her cheek. Alex moves to swipe it away, but I'm already kneeling on the bed beside her, gathering her dainty body in my arms so I can collect whatever parts of herself she'll grant me. If tears are the only thing I can hold onto, I'll take it.

She buries her face in my chest as I lay down beside her, gathering her in my arms, which is exactly where it belongs. Two heads on one pillow.

"You disappeared!" she protests into my shirt. "You've been gone for like, a week? Two weeks? The second the marriage stuff got real, you split."

I throw my head back, looking up at the ceiling to curse my stupidity. "I was building ye a house. Ye said ye wanted me to ask ye properly for your hand, and I didn't. Tha's where I was, building ye a house so I could ask for your hand the right way."

"What? That's not a thing." Another tear falls onto my chest directly over my heart. "To ask for someone's hand, it's a simple conversation, which we never had. You left. If you didn't go off to be with another woman, then I don't understand."

She feels too good in my arms, so I don't mind it when Justice answers for me. "Shifter custom is for the lad to provide shelter before asking a lass for her hand. Most of the time it's a burrow or something, but since you're fae, tha must be why it took longer, since you'd need an actual structure to live in. You're really mated with a fae, Brother?" His eyes cut to Lily. "You're Hannah? All this time, it was ye Salem was in love with?"

I grumble at him. "How quick do ye assume a man can build a house by himself? Those things take time. I was working day and night to get it finished up so I could marry Lily." Obviously tha's what I was doing. "How did I get tha wrong?"

"You don't have to build me a house!" Lily blurts out. "All I want is to be with you."

It's the best thing I've ever heard a woman say to me. The words are so sweet, I have to kiss the mouth tha said them. Maybe my lips crash against hers with too much passion, but tha doesn't seem to bother her. Her fingers tangle in my hair and tug, just the way I like it. I need to taste her tongue, to feel her heart race against mine as our chests press together. I don't want anything between us, but her clothes stay on because we have an audience who doesn't know when to leave a lad alone with his lass.

"Marry me," I beg between kisses.

Tears are streaming down her face faster than I can clear them with my thumbs. "I've been in love with you for so long, Salem."

Alex squeezes my shoulder, inserting himself in a moment I'm too content in to push him away. "Welcome to the family, Brother."

Finally Alex slips out the door behind Justice, giving us

the space to promise each other all the things I thought were implied. "It's always been ye. Only ye. I meant everything I said before. I don't know how I got it so wrong."

She bites down on my lower lip, stirring things in me I don't know how to turn off. "That's why I was so upset when Justice told me you had a girlfriend. It all felt so real to me, everything you said about coming into the pub just to see me." When I tip my head back, she kisses a line down my throat, driving me mad as her leg slips between my thighs. "You wrote down everything I ever said to you in the pub on napkins, and you keep them with you. I didn't understand how you could have those napkins and belong to someone else."

"Tha's because I only belong to ye. I should've told ye where I was going. I thought ye knew." I kiss her harder because I can't not. "Ye wanted a proper proposal." I cradle her head in the crook of my arm, so I can kiss her however I like.

"And then you disappeared without proposing!"

"Aye. To give ye a proper proposal!" I chuckle at the mishap, but the sound turns into a low rumble when her fingers unhook the buttons on my shirt. Her leg moves from between mine and curls up and around my waist. Her fingers trail down the row of buttons, undoing me completely. Her lips and hips fuse to mine, and I know there's no turning back now.

She owns my body, which sinks back into the mattress so she can undress me however she likes. She straddles my hips, and I can safely say I've never seen a prettier sight. I can't believe it's my body tha pleases her, me who makes those torturous little noises come out as she grinds her warmth over mine. My eyes roll back as she takes what she needs from me, and gives me more pleasure than I ever thought possible.

I can't stop staring in wonder at the woman who's looking at me like I'm the thing she wants. Salem Butcher, who never drew out a soft word from a woman now gets a queen stroking his chest and hooking her thumbs in his undershorts. Salem Butcher, who only wanted one thing for himself, finally has her kissing a trail down his chest and toward his stomach.

When her tongue sweeps over the dip in my hips, I can't help the strangled cry that fills the room. She's torturing me, and I love it. "Marry me!" I beg her again.

She smirks, her lashes framing those doe eyes tha've always done me in. "Do you think I do this for just anyone?"

Despite the selfish parts of me tha throw a tantrum because I'm making her stop, my arms pull her up my body so her lips are an inch away from mine. I need to see her eyes up close, make sure nothing comes between us ever again—not even a misunderstanding. "Lilya Klein, will ye marry me?"

Her eyes glisten with longing I've needed to see up close. It's there, the promise of permanence I never thought would belong to me. "Yes, Salem. Let's get married."

There's no holding me back as I attack the lips tha say

such perfect things. She's melting into my body, my arm wrapping around her to keep her so close, it's like we're one body.

Of all the things I've always wanted, when Lily pledges herself to me, I know I'm about to get the life I never thought I'd be allowed to touch.

But she lets me touch her. And for the next two hours, she lets me do whatever I want.

24

A DRINKING PROBLEM

DESTINO

Dinner is a strange affair, what with Ronin and me sipping on our blood drinks and Queen Butcher in a long dressing gown and robe. She gave birth to Salem and Justice, so I don't know why her height always surprises me. It's been a fair few years since she's been upright, so I chalk my staring up to the fact that I'm unaccustomed to seeing her around. "Are you sure you're alright, my queen?" I ask her when she looks as if holding her fork is too arduous a task.

Her gray lashes lift as she smiles. "'My queen'? I rather like the sound of a vampire claiming me as his queen."

"Well, that's what you are, right? That's what we're building toward? If King Fairbucks weren't so very stubborn about it all, I would call him my king. As it is," I lift my glass to Queen Kloe, who dips her head in my direction. "My queens."

Ronin studies me before he speaks. "It'll take some time

to get used to that. But you're right, Son. We will all belong to each other, which is as it should be. All that aside, perhaps we should talk about the elephant in the room."

"She's my mate," Salem confesses, his chin lifted in defiance of convention. "Lily and I, we… I don't know how it happened, but we're mated." He points to his blue eye so everyone can note the difference that's subtle but significant.

"Is your eye blue?" Queen Butcher asks with a gasp.

Justice hangs his head. "Jays, rub it in tha I didn't notice a change tha obvious."

Salem rubs the nape of his neck. "Aye. They changed when Lily and I were… So tha's what we're dealing with."

"How is this possible?" Queen Butcher was pale before, but now she looks positively gaunt. The food at the table as gone from interesting to ornamental as everyone forgets their appetite. "Some trick of the fae?"

Alex, Salem and I all stiffen at the affront, but Alex speaks up first, since Lily's always been content letting people say whatever awful things they like about her. "No fae in the history of the world has ever been able to trick a shifter into mating. If anything, it only makes Lily's life more complicated. The two of them have been taken with each other for years before this came about."

"It's nature." I'm not sure why I'm speaking up, but it's been marinating in my brain for some time now. "Destiny decided change wasn't happening fast enough, so it's helped us along. Once the fae and the shifters see the intensity of the bond between Salem and Lily, they'll understand nature doesn't need us to be separate. Fate is very much pushing us together."

Ronin raises his glass to me, leaning back in his seat as he takes it all in. "Well said, Son."

Justice massages his forehead. "How exactly are ye supposed to be mated to a woman ye share with two other lads? It's not uncommon for a shifter to tear the throat out of someone who looks at his mate like he shouldn't. This is all going to fall apart if ye attack Destino or Alexavier."

Salem's jaw is set, but he has the look of bearing guilt to him, which isn't what I want for my best friend to feel when he announces to his family such a huge life event. "I've seen her with Des and Alex. It was hard, but we're managing. They protect what I love, so I can handle it."

Justice offers up a derisive scoff, but I suppose only time will tell if Salem's right. Judging by the way he doesn't push away Alex's arm that's draped over the back of Lily's chair, I'd say we're well on our way to making this work.

"Speaking of delightful little hiccups," Ronin says, his eyes on the fine crystal they broke out for us. "That wasn't the elephant in the room I was referring to. It seems we have a bit of a bigger problem on our hands than an unlikely coupling."

Justice's elbows are on the table, his head in his hands as he glares at Ronin. "Bigger than a shifter mated to a fae? Bigger than my brother mated to a lass who's married to his two best mates? Grand. Let's hear it."

"There are many things our bigotry has sheltered us from, namely interspecies mating, which might happen more and more in the future, given all the changes we're making. Once that border comes down, we'll be in for all sorts of surprises. Best put our cards on the table, yes?"

Queen Butcher sighs. "Why do I get the feeling the roof's about to cave in on our heads? Out with it, King Ronin."

He waves off her proper address. "Do call me Ronin, Magdeena. You've seen me naked. I hardly think we need to bother with formalities, given all that's transpiring."

Salem and Justice let out cries of horror, matching my own shock as my drink sloshes down my fingers. "What are you on about? Since when have you two seen each other naked?"

Ronin sniggers at Queen Butcher's snarl. Though, judging by her reddening cheeks, Ronin's not lying. "Is tha never talking about it again?"

"It's true?" Justice looks like he's about to be sick.

Queen Butcher rests her forehead in her hand, unable to look at her sons. Instead, she glowers at Ronin. "It was ages ago. Your father had passed, and Ronin came to give his condolences to our family and our people. I was griev-ing, and we were very, very drunk."

I scoff. "Come now. It's not as if it requires copious amounts of alcohol to find a vampire attractive. Well done to both of you." I lift my glass to them, which draws a bleat of chagrin from Queen Butcher and a snigger from Grand-father, the cheeky bastard.

Justice looks as if he suddenly wishes for the childish option of shoving cotton into his ears.

Queen Kloe giggles into her martini. "Magdeena, I had no idea."

Queen Butcher's teeth grind through her words. "Because it was supposed to be a secret."

Ronin tsks her. "Now, now, Maggie. Don't act as if you regret it. I know I don't." He toasts her, and Salem's upper lip curls.

Queen Butcher huffs, her eyes on the ceiling. "Did ye have a point, Ronin? Or are ye running your gob only to upset me?"

"You know, you'd think that would be enough motivation for me, but I actually did have a grander point. Salem and Lilya mating is just one surprise we've missed out on that our people could have been experiencing for years. There's a peculiar development not many of my people are aware of, because the dividing lines between our territories kept them from such discoveries. Now that the borders will be coming down, it bears mentioning."

Justice shakes his head at Ronin. "Do ye always speak in riddles, old man? Spit it out already."

Ronin chuckles at Justice's frustration. "When Destino almost died after they escaped the Stone Graveyard, he was nearing starvation. From what I understand, things were pretty dire."

I can't believe he's bringing this up in mixed company. I set down my glass and lean forward in my seat. "That's private, Ronin. They won't understand."

"They won't understand that your life means more than decorum? I highly doubt that." Ronin gives them all a lighthearted scoff meant to communicate that of course they care about my life, even if he knows it's a stretch. "Lilya's Green Lightning had run out, so she let Destino feed directly from her to save his life."

Yes, to save my life. But she let me feed off of her this morning just for fun. Heat floods my veins when I picture her wanton expression in my mind, her body twisting in the sheets in total surrender to whatever I want. I love when she's completely open, arching beneath me because the rush of my teeth in her neck feels just that good to her.

Judging by the blush in her cheeks as she locks eyes with me across the table, I can tell she's reliving the same erotic moment neither of us have the sense to be ashamed of. Maybe we should, but it feels too good for us to stop.

The horrified gasps from Justice and Queen Butcher aren't unexpected. "Tha's…" I can tell Justice wants to say we're disgusting or vile, but he can't bring himself to tell Lily she should've let me die rather than do something that felt dangerous. They don't know I could never hurt her.

I love her.

Ronin's unbothered by the tension he's single-handedly creating. "Another chap had the same problem ages ago. He drank from a fae messenger. Understand, he was too out of his mind with thirst to stop. The fae didn't have Green Lightning in his system, so when the vampire drank his fill, he didn't understand why his head was splitting so badly, he couldn't see straight."

My mouth goes dry. "Headaches like mine?"

Ronin swirls the blood in his cup. "Indeed. The pain

drove him mad. It wasn't until moments before he drove a silver dagger through his temple that he confessed of drinking directly from a fae." His eyes flick to Lily, who chews on her lower lip like she's afraid to put food in her mouth. "Seeing Destino's headaches when he's parted from Lilya confirms it for me. Lilya and Destino are bound."

All the heat in my body leaves me. "What are you on about? That's not a thing. There's no bodily punishment nature enacts if a vampire drinks from a person." My goblet crashes too hard to the table.

Ronin's voice drops. "In my mum's journals, there was an account of this as well. She mentioned something over and over called 'the madness.' I suspected this might be it, but now I'm certain. You've bonded, and I'm not terribly certain of all that will come to mean. But I do know a few things from Mum's notes and that poor vampire's suicide." His eyes lock on Lily's even though he's addressing me. "The pain of being separate from Lilya will drive you mad, Destino. If a tolerance can be built up, or the tether might be lengthened over time, I do not know. What I am certain of is that the two of you must stay in close proximity, or the Drexdenberg throne will be in jeopardy." When Lily covers her mouth through a gasp, he turns to address her. "I will not see Destino drive a stake through his temple because the pain of being apart from you is too great." His gaze is piercing Lily, who is shaken, but doesn't shy away from the challenge. I love that about her.

"Of course not," Lily agrees.

I sit straighter, scrambling for a plan. "How long will

the bond last? If I stop drinking from my wife, surely it will fade." The moment the words leave me, I realize they're the wrong ones. I don't want to stop. I'm not sure I'm capable.

Salem and Alex know we haven't stopped. Salem insisted on watching the whole thing, making sure I didn't truly hurt her. It was strange, make no mistake, but the taste of Lily is so divine that I'll take what I can get. If Salem has to be part of our time together, so be it. She tastes like... she tastes like fresh air smells. She's pure desire, and there are precious few pure things in this world anymore.

Ronin turns in his seat, giving me his full attention. "Surely you aren't still drinking from her."

I'm going to be king next year, so squirming under scrutiny isn't something I'm supposed to do. "Well, I mean, not all the time. But on occasion. It's..." I reach for the proper words, but I'm thinking the right thing is for the earth to open up and swallow me whole rather than confess to the room how stimulating the whole thing is.

Lily saves me, as she always manages to. "It's incredible, and it's my choice. I don't care if it's weird. It's between Des and me, and Salem and Lexi. The list of people who should weigh in on our arrangement ends there."

Ronin's mouth drops open as her declaration stirs something primal in me. She's not ashamed of me or our strange connection. I love the defiant look to her when she claims me without equivocation.

Ronin straightens. "Well, that is a development I wasn't expecting. I'll admit, it used to take much to shock me, but it seems you keep delivering surprise after surprise, my darling."

I hate it when he talks to her like that.

"If we stop, how long with the bond last?"

Ronin drags his hand over his mouth and down his chin as he calculates all he knows and measures it against the inevitable. "The vampire who killed himself only drank the one time, and he endured the agony for two months before he took his life. In Mum's journals, there was no end mentioned, though they were quite cryptic."

Silence drapes the table like a damper on an already grim evening. I don't want to say the thing we're all thinking, but it's there all the same. "Lily can't live in Drexdenberg with me all the time. I'm going to rule next year, which means I'll need to be with my people for the most part."

Alex shakes his head, his eyes wide as they take in the mess before him. "I lived without her for too many years. Our bond isn't like yours, but I'm not going to marry her and then simply visit her once a month or however often I can get away. And if we start a family someday..."

Dread coils in my stomach of the problems that didn't need to be, but now very much are.

"No," Salem rules, his voice gruff. "I mated with her first. My tie to her isn't something tha can be undone. And I'm not a *future* leader; I'm *currently* leading the military in Jacoba. I can't move to Drexdenberg."

It's a strange sight to watch Salem in love. It's like watching a rhinoceros tap dance. He jerks her seat toward his and slaps his thigh. It would look bossy, but for the insecure plea in his eyes.

Lily obliges his caveman nature and slides over to sit atop his thigh. He's being childish, but she permits him to claim her publicly like this because she's kind and he's a right baby. "It's alright, Salem. We'll figure this out."

She's dainty and slender, swallowed by his bulk. If it was anyone but Salem, I'd be worried about him breaking her, but Salem's so careful with her body; I don't get too ruffled at the sight. Her arm loops around him so she can tease the small hairs at the nape of his neck. He shivers, and finally begins to calm down.

She's so good for him.

Ronin's gaze cuts from me to Alex, and then lands on Salem. "Yes, it looks like we definitely have a problem."

25

WHITE DRESS

LILYA

My white dress isn't as tolerant of the dirt as I am. I didn't mean to get dust on it, but the lace collects the trappings of the road like nothing else. "Hold still. I'll get this out." Lexi always makes me snicker when he fusses over cute things like stains. As if that's the thing to focus on today.

The white dress isn't part of the shifter marriage ritual, but as I'm fae, Lexi insisted I look the part of the blushing fairy bride.

"I hardly think that matters," I tell him as Justice's voice booms out across the land. I'm gripping the edge of the steps that lead up to the raised platform where Justice, Salem, Queen Kloe and Ronin are standing. I can see the tightness in their backs as they position themselves with a foot of distance between each of them—separate but very much together. I try to reach for a wry smile to give to Lexi. "The people are most likely going to throw mud at me the second it's all announced, so keeping me spotless is kind of a pipe dream."

"They are not," Des offers as his arm coils around my waist. It's a sweet lie, but a lie nonetheless.

It's just the three of us at the base of the steps with Queen Butcher behind us, hidden behind the platform that faces the whole of the Jacoba territory. Every shifter is in attendance, no doubt hoping for fantastic news, only to soon be let down by a devastating blow that they're now stuck with me.

"They're going to hate me, hate the new direction of things, and hate Salem because of me. I know it's probably too much to ask, but I was hoping just one of my weddings wouldn't be protested and despised. Weddings are supposed to be happy occasions."

Lexi's hand is gentle as he turns my chin so he can look deep into my eyes. "Are you happy?"

"I'm happy I'm marrying Salem, yes."

"Then that'll have to do for now."

Queen Butcher hasn't fidgeted through the entire event thus far. She stands hidden with us, but a couple feet behind me below the platform, listening to our exchanges with tight lips that curve into a small smile every now and then. "It does my heart good to hear tha," she tells us. "Tell him more often than ye think ye need to. My Salem deserves to know he's loved."

"Of course," I say with a slight bow.

Lexi fixes his eyes on Justice's back. "That's your cue," he says to Queen Butcher.

"Cheers, Prince Alexavier." Queen Butcher is tall and regal, with a jaw as stern as her sons', but with a steady gentleness to her eyes that every person would want in their ruler. She pauses at the base of the steps, reaching out to grip my icy fingers. "Let them throw mud if they must. But keep your chin high and your eyes fixed on the future. This is but a moment. A moment doesn't make ye, and a moment can't destroy ye if ye understand what's important."

"Yes, your majesty," I say, inclining my head to her again.

"Mammy," she corrects me with a wink. "Even if ye weren't about to marry my son, I would ask ye to call me tha."

I like her so very much. Her blue velvet robes are regal, to be sure, but it's the way she carries herself with her shoulders back and head high as she moves up the steps that convinces me she's a born leader.

Justice's speech swells, ending in the announcement that their queen is well again, and ready to reclaim the throne her sons kept warm for her.

The thousands of animal howls and verbal cheers are so deafening, I wince against Lexi, who takes care not to mess up my hair as he presses my ear to his chest to muffle the noise. Des' hand finds my back, and I'm fairly certain my knees are shaking so badly, I would be in danger of falling if they weren't surrounding me.

This is where I need to be, even if they don't want me. I need to get the shifters consistent access to water. I want to do everything in my power to heal relations between the shifters and the fae so Jacoba's land has a chance at blossoming.

The part that's making me tremble is that Salem will be hated on his wedding day. I might be part of the plan that redeems his land, but I'm also going to be the one who makes his followers turn on him. I want to marry Salem so very badly, to belong to him as much as he's always belonged in my heart. But part of me knows I'm the waitress from the seedy pub in Neutral Territory, and he's an actual prince. He commands an entire army, and I didn't even have the authority to change a menu item. How he ever noticed me, scarred and small as I am, is beyond me.

And now the entire shifter territory is going to spot how much I don't deserve to be near someone as incredible as Salem.

When the cheering dies down after a full five minutes of jubilation, I hold onto Lexi so tight, I'm afraid I might draw blood and ruin his white pants and dress shirt. Queen Butcher greets her people, and though her tenor remains steady, there's no mistaking the swell of love she has for them. I feel that same wave rise up in me, and as much as I'm able, outsider that I am, I want to belong to these warriors, these cast-outs.

Queen Butcher's voice booms out across the land, sounding a mix of regal and loving. "The lass who brought me back to life and captured my tormentor shall be given in marriage to my son. She loved our family and our people enough to question how I landed in my coma. She stopped at nothing, taking great personal sacrifice upon herself, to bring me back to ye."

The buildup of making me sound like some impressive person is normally something I would cringe away from, but I absorb her gratitude, amplified as it is. They're about to see me for the first time and will need to hold tight to Queen Butcher's acceptance of me if they're ever going to let me help them.

"Salem has never been questioned in his ability to lead our army, and has proved he's capable of trust in this decision to select a lass. I can assure ye, she's gifted in standing tall by his side."

It's almost my turn to let the entire nation down and piss everyone off at the same time. My palms are sweating and the flash of desire to run away from the stage and all it represents fills my entire body. It's not until Queen Butcher says my name and I don't move that Salem turns to see what the holdup is.

I want to go to Salem, but I can't. So I freeze, separating myself from the destiny I've chosen.

26

OUR PEOPLE

LILYA

I'm the holdup. I'm the chicken. I'm the one stock-still while my husbands are gently urging me to move up the steps. I can't do it. I want to marry Salem, of course, but a third territory despising me for my love feels like something beyond what I'm capable of handling in this exact moment.

Des and Lexi step back when Ronin moves toward us, trots down the platform steps away from the view of the throngs of shifters, and flicks his wrist so we have some semblance of privacy from the guys and guards. Even Benny, Ronin's most trusted guard, steps back. "Darling, are you quite alright?"

Ronin can handle my fear without feeling personally rejected or attacked, so I don't hold back the panic in my eyes. "I think I'm having a stroke or something! I want to marry Salem, but they're going to…"

And now I'm hyperventilating. Fantastic.

Ronin holds my face like he knows how, focusing my increasingly blurring vision in that hypnotic way he's mastered. "This one is real for you, yes?"

I'm running out of words, so I nod emphatically. "I didn't know Des, and Lexi was my friend first, so that wasn't too big a leap. But this? Now it's here, this incredible thing, offering itself to me like I'm the kind of girl who should get what she wants." I shake my head at myself, disgusted with everything I am.

Ronin brings my body tight to his so our words stay just between us. His lips tickle my ear, pushing the rest of the world out of focus. My heart is pounding, but Ronin's is steady, so I cling to the life raft. "There is no crowd. There is no crown. There is only your heart and Salem's. Do you love him?"

Desperation to be near my brooding, bulky, sexy prince fills every fiber of my being, but still I can't move. Each step along this journey has been expected to be taken without hesitation, but all that cumulative jumping off the cliff has brought me to a place where I'm too nervous to take another step.

"Do you love him?" Ronin asks again, my knees trembling while he holds me. His dapper suit is never disheveled, and despite the potential disaster we're walking into, neither is he. He curves a finger around one of my pinned curls.

I picture Salem's face, never smoothly shaved, hiding that sliver of a smile he gets every now and then when he thinks no one's looking. But I see him. I see his moments of happiness, and I truly want to be one. I want to be the thing that makes him smile.

"I do," I confess. "I love Salem so much, I'm not sure my heart can handle it. I love him so badly, my insides feel hollow when he's gone. I love him, Ronin, and I'm not sure I'll ever be able to cure it."

Ronin's smile lifts my cheek in time with his. He kisses the spot near my ear and whispers, "Then go get him."

Just like that, a switch flips in my heart, untethering me from the spot I've been clinging to in life that promises hope can only bring pain. I gather the front of my lace dress up and make my way up the steps, slowly revealing myself to the people. First they glimpse my lavender hair, then my too-white face, then my bridal gown. I can see their collective confusion and dismay that I'm not the tanned Jacoba princess they ordered. My heart is hammering so loudly, I can barely hear the outcry and the animal howls that are no doubt calling for my head.

I'm supposed to stand in the center of the platform with the queen, Justice, Salem, Kloe and Ronin behind me. Lexi and Des are to join them in the background, standing with them to make our kingdoms look like a united front. We rehearsed it all, but the plan flies out of my head at the sight of Salem in a suit, all shaved and bathed with a note of need in his eyes when he sees me. I don't stand in the center, but beeline straight for him. My ring needs to feel his heart, to know for sure that all we're about to promise each other will remain true until the end.

"Sorry it took me so long," I tell him, unsure if I mean

just now, or the winding road it took us to get to this moment.

Salem gazes at me like I'm something amazing, something breakable, something precious. "I would have waited forever."

I'm supposed to pause for Queen Butcher to give the next bit of her speech, but I can't. I'm afraid that if I put off kissing Salem another second, something in me will scream so loud, part of my very soul might die off completely. I surprise a shocked noise from him as I stand on my toes, my arms looping around his neck so I can kiss him how I like to. His arms encircle my frame with a chuckle that vibrates from my lips all the way to my toes.

Finally, my knees steady. My thighs calm their quaking. I love the sound of his happiness. It melts into me and fills my dark places with hope I promised the world I've never needed. His lips are soft just at the moment I know the world is about to turn rough. I love him for becoming my soft thing, for the arms that cradle without coveting, for the lips that promise without words that even when the world falls apart, we will always have each other.

There is no applause. There is no outrage. Even though the field is filled with tens of thousands of shifters, there is utter and total silence that consumes whatever reaction they may have had at the ready.

Many turn their heads away, unable to hide their disgust. Des and Lexi frame us, lending their political weight to ensure the territory knows of their support.

Queen Butcher explains the lengthy story of our plan to

unite the territories. She doesn't apologize for or diminish my marriage to Des. She doesn't tighten up at the mention of my marriage to Lexi. She's a woman who isn't afraid of her own voice, and I love her for it.

"So when Salem wanted to marry Lilya, I worried her plan was more important than our people. After watching her care for my sons and bring me back to ye at great personal sacrifice, I can assure ye, tha has not been the case. Though she is new to our people, she loves us enough to risk her safety to bring the three heads of the territories together to barter a peace agreement. She saw an injustice —tha Jacoba was being forgotten—and sacrificed everything to give us a brighter future."

Ronin steps forward. This is where he's to say his part about the specifics of the treaty we signed without King Fairbucks' knowledge, but before he begins, he hooks his arm around my waist and brings me to the front of the stage beside him, making it look as though the two of us are delivering this message together. I mean, we decided on it together, but it's clear to me he needs Jacoba to understand that I'm a decisionmaker, not just a girl in a fancy dress.

Ronin's voice projects with a firm power across the mix of animal and human heads. "Queen Kloe and Prince Alexavier are committed to helping the citizens of Jacoba not just survive, but thrive. In exchange for tearing down your borders and sharing your plumapples, they are going to assemble a team of fae that will set up and maintain enough wells to ensure every shifter never thirsts again.

They will sprout food-bearing plants and make your fields green again, as they were in the days of your forefathers."

Only Ronin can get away with using fancy words like "forefathers" and get everyone to agree with him.

Ronin's unwrinkled and unruffled disposition is delivered with ease as he explains the treaty between the fae and vampires as well, but his arm tightens around me. Only I can tell that he's worried. I can read between the lines of his self-possessed smile and neatly fastened bow tie. Though the entire territory is picking apart every word, every movement, my body can't help but curve toward his, my truth-seeking ring finding its way to his heart, where it knows it will find layers and layers of deception.

But I let him lie to the world and tell them it'll all be okay.

I let him lie to me, because I need the hope, even if it's a wish at this point.

The moment my form clings to his, my stomach tight to his hip, Ronin's voice grows more impassioned. "Your future queen will not sit by as Queen Butcher, the fae Fairbucks rulers, and I have done for too many years." His fingers grip my hip, digging in to let only me know his confidence is riddled with cracks. "Lilya will put her life in danger, stand before you and tell us to our faces that we must change, or we'll lose all we love about the territories we're fighting so hard to defend. I do not wish to lose what I love, so I welcome the shifters into Drexdenberg. In one week's time, it will become our law that any vampire caught attacking a shifter will receive the same punishment they would receive for turning on one of their kin. The high premium I should have placed on your lives long ago will be proclaimed, and all I ask is that you take your time forgiving me for my cowardice, for my shortsighted behavior in thinking shifters would never want more than the life and the land you have."

Ronin's other arm brushes down the curve of my side for the whole territory to see, turning his body so there's no way around it—we're embracing, holding each other together while we place ourselves square in the center of the target. Together we brace ourselves for the arrows we know are coming. My hand remains over his heart, where, for this moment in history, it belongs.

I know Des doesn't like the sight of me in Ronin's arms, but this is where I need to be, so I stay in harm's way for what I hope is the greater good. When I feel a hand on my shoulder, I'm not surprised to see Des, though I am relieved that his hand has recently regained some of its functionality.

I'm also not shocked when Lexi steps forward to stand with us. It's when Salem comes forward, taking my hand, that I truly worry we've gone too far off-book. Salem doesn't address the people publicly all too often, from what I've been told. He doesn't like to talk much, but I can see his chest puffing with something to say as he claims me as his in front of the entire territory. "Lilya Klein is my mate. As much as ye respect me, you'll stand by her."

That's when murmuring and gasps multiply and splinter out over the field.

Salem doesn't back down. "I don't understand how it happened, but it did. So if anyone is confused about what fate wants for Jacoba, here we are. See tha she belongs to our people, and should be protected as your princess."

Queen Butcher's voice echoes out over the crowd. "Jacoba, your future!" Then she gestures to Salem and me.

Of all the things I expected to happen, I am truly shocked when the entire territory puts their confusion and questions on hold to obey their queen. Heads lower and knees are taken, and in the middle of it, no one is more shocked than me.

There are no arrows. There are no protests. There is only respect for the journey that led us here, and the years of work still ahead of us.

I love my family, and looking out at the sea of shifters, I realize that these are our people, and I love them, too.

27

NEW HOME, NEW WORLD

LILYA

*I*f I had a coin for every time Ronin drew a glower from me, I'd be a very rich woman. Though, as I now have access to three treasuries, maybe that's true regardless of how many times he pisses me off. "I'm not useless, you know."

"Indeed. I think you're confusing 'useless' with 'treasured'. I don't want you moving furniture into the castle because you're to be queen. It's not proper. Benny can get that."

I brush some dirt off my jeans and then face him, arms akimbo. Only Ronin wears a three-piece suit to help someone move. "It wouldn't be proper to work for what I have? This is my house too, you know."

Ronin looks at the structure with a sigh of discontent, not even romanced by the overpowering scent of freshly-hewn wood. "You're right, it's hardly a castle. It is more like a house. I mean, it's only two stories tall. You should have one floor for each husband, at least. And where are the parapets? This is ridiculous." He taps his foot to the base board. It's a lighter color than the dark wood floor, and his nose crinkles as if the simple touch offends him.

Benny picks up the box before I can protest, because he's just that good.

I try not to let too much exasperation show, but honestly, it's been all day with these two. "It's the first project the three territories are working on together, and it's a far sight bigger than the apartment I lived in most of my life, so I'm not about to complain."

"It doesn't even have a fountain."

"You are such a snob."

Ronin smiles at me in that lazy way that always charms me. "Darling, that's what you adore about me."

I open up a box at my feet to make sure it's in the correct room. I don't look forward to going down the stairs again if this is in the wrong spot. "I'm not sure you understand what 'adore' means."

"I'm not sure you understand what 'queen' means. Let me educate you." He slides the box away from me with his foot and loops my hand around his bicep. He tilts his head in greeting to one of the fae servants who will be helping tend the gardens. "A queen serves her people by enacting fair policies. She, in turn, is served by the people who are grateful for her care. Her enemies are locked away."

We take a deep breath together. The fact that both Vera and my father are locked away, far from spreading their hate to the world, brings me solace no throne ever could.

Ronin kisses my forehead. "A queen is above, and I will not see you compromised after all our hard work to get here."

"It's been a crazy year; I'll grant you that."

"Are you ready for Destino's coronation next month? It will be your coronation as well. You've been our princess for so long, but now you'll officially be queen."

My stomach roils. "Don't talk like that. I'm already nervous enough."

Ronin flicks his wrist, like life is so very easy. "What's the point of nerves? The worst of it all is behind us, darling. The shifters took to the change so peaceably, I curse myself for not starting with them. The fae are too concerned with image to be considered the brutes who stir up dissention so overtly. They're falling in line quite nicely these days."

"And the vampires? Are you really going to lie to me and say it's all been smooth sailing? Because I gotta tell you, I don't even need this truth-seeking ring to spot the hole in that story."

Ronin leans in closer with his charming smile that never fully fades these days. "What's the fun of smooth sailing? I prefer the thrill of adventure when you don't quite know the outcome."

"You're a real pill, you know that? Drexdenberg hates me. They resent Des for this change, and you know it."

"Ah, but you're forgetting one very important thing."

"And what's that?"

"I don't care." At my epic eye roll, Ronin laughs. "What?

I truly don't. It's the medicine they need, so they'll take it and be all the better for it. Ever since I raised the punishments for interspecies attacks, there have been far fewer incidents of vampires stirring up trouble. And it's not as if you'll have to see your dissenters all the time." He motions around with a grin. "Tell me I'm brilliant for suggesting your new castle be built in Neutral Territory. Tell me I'm your king."

"Until next month, you're my king. My eccentric, dangerous, reckless king." I pause to fasten the ends of his bowtie he always toys with. "Then you're my court jester."

Ronin feigns a mortal wound, clutching his chest. "I'll always be your something. Your eccentric, dangerous, reckless something." He touches my nose so cutely, I almost forget how annoying he's been. "And you'll always be my adorable someone. I'll tolerate nothing less."

"Mm," I murmur, my eyes cutting sideways to his grin. "Starting our new regime by building a castle in Neutral Territory wasn't your worst idea, I'll grant you that. I love that we don't have to be apart. The guys are so happy living together."

"You've designated a room for me when I come to visit you, yes?"

"Of course. Feel free to decorate that as obnoxiously as you like. What would a castle be without my kings?"

Ronin frowns at the dark wood-hewn floor. "Calling this place a castle really isn't accurate. Once I'm retired, I'll see to making this place truly shine. This wall color should be gold, not bronze. Can't have my queen slumming it, yes?"

"Yes, what an impoverished castle this is. You're ridiculous."

Ronin ignores my sarcasm, as he always does. "I'm yours, darling, so take me as I am and enjoy the ride."

Des comes into the room and sets down a box. "I really hate it when you talk to my wife like that. I get that she's your only friend, but it's creepy. You're old. And you're related now." He jabs a finger in my direction. "My wife, not yours. I'm the one who took her last name, not you."

Ronin smirks. "Yes, yes. Brilliant idea of Salem's, truly. All three of you giving up your last names to take hers was a sweet gesture, though 'Destino Karamathian Klein' will take some getting used to."

It's not often Des gets overtly territorial. I move closer to him, eyeing the box of books in his arms. "Are you thinking this should be the study? Because I was kind of hoping the study could be on the same floor as Fiora's bedroom. I don't want her going up and down the stairs all the time. It's bad for her knees."

Des shakes his head. "I started setting up a room for her downstairs. This here is down the hall from our bedroom. These are baby books," he says of the box in his arms. "If we board up the windows, it would be the perfect nursery. Look at how much space the baby will have to crawl and learn to walk."

Salem ducks his head in, sniffing the air and scrutinizing the corners. "I'll set to filing down tha sharp edge over there." He jerks his chin to the window sill that's too new to have a speck of dust on it yet.

I hold up my hands, as I always do when the guys let their imaginations run away with them. "I'm not even pregnant, and I don't plan on it anytime soon. We don't need a nursery yet."

"Crib in the far corner?" Des asks Salem, as if I hadn't said a word in protest.

Salem nods. "Aye. I'll start building it this week. Don't want our wee babe to sleep in something I haven't built. Can't trust it otherwise."

"Baby? Are you pregnant?" Lexi's voice comes into the room before he does, his countenance matching his excited tone when he bounds in and throws his arms around me, lifting my feet off the ground.

He's so cute, I almost feel bad for bursting his bubble. "I'm nothing like pregnant, and you three are nothing like listening." I kiss Lexi's smile as it fades. "I told you, not until we've settled into our rhythm. There've been too many cross-species attacks. I'm not about to bring a baby into this mess."

Salem jerks up a box with a grumpy frown, as if I've just told him he's fat or something. "I'll have Justice and Mammy make another announcement to the people, going over the punishments for assault."

"It's not your people, and you know it." I try not to eye Ronin. It's not his fault the vampires are having a harder time adjusting to the change.

Lexi sets my feet back down. "I'll see to tightening up

security around the castle."

Ronin sighs heavily, his hands in his pockets. "I suppose I could post more soldiers in the common areas. Even though I'm nearly ready to hand off the crown, I guess that wouldn't be too difficult."

I tilt my head at him, not holding back an ounce of my sass. "How magnanimous of you to do your job while it's still your job."

His eyes twinkle at me, which bespeaks a mischief I'm never ready for. "Yes, but in a month, *this* will be my job." He sweeps me up in a quick-step dance I can barely keep up with, surprising laughter from me, as he always does.

The guys are not amused.

Ronin stops our dance after a few beats. "You can finish unpacking without your queen, gentlemen. I'll return her in a moment. We've still much to discuss." He hooks his arm around my hip and leads me out of the room.

"What's on your mind, Ronin?"

"Only everything. Mostly how to distract you from doing commoner chores." At my scoff, he concedes, holding up his hand. "Very well. I do have something real that could use your input. I'm not sure how best to integrate more shifters and fae into vampire territory. We're still three separate territories, even though the borders have been torn down."

I run my hand along the wall that's been painted a soft bronze color. It doesn't take away from the fresh wood cabin-y look, but dresses up the simple structure to make it lavish while still modest. "I suppose we could offer a stipend for cost of living or free lodging for any who wants to move to Drexdenberg. That might encourage people to move outside their comfort zones."

"Brilliant. I'll put through the necessary orders tonight. Let's offer that to Jacoba, not Faveda. The fae are too delicate for Drexdenberg just yet."

We pause at a window, our conversation stopping when the moon greets us. It's as if the glowing sphere has been waiting to show off only for people who will truly appreciate its magnificence. It's so huge tonight, and from this angle, it seems to fill half the sky.

"I think this will be my favorite spot in the house," I say aloud, unable to tear my eyes from the orb that seems to understand my concerns for the Queendom.

Queendom. Not three territories, but one Queendom. Never thought I'd see the day.

"As far as spots go, you could've chosen worse. Perhaps we should get you a chair just there, so you can enjoy it as long as you like. Spots like these are important so you don't lose perspective."

"What's the perspective I'm not supposed to lose?"

Ronin gazes at the moon by my side, his eyes wistful instead of teasing. "That not everything needs your hand upon it to make it turn. Some things will always be good, no matter how badly we try to sully them with our fighting and hatred. Sometimes it's hard to find that one good thing, yet you're barely moved in, and you've already found it. But that seems to be your nature—finding the one good thing wherever you go."

I straighten his bowtie. "Must be how I found you."

His eyes darken. "I am not good, no matter how much you wish it so."

"Are you happy like that?"

He pauses, and I can tell he's turning my words over, considering them from all angles. "I'm me like that. When you look at me how you are right now, it stirs something strange in me."

"Look at you like what?"

Ronin inhales a long breath, his eyes drinking in the scope of my face like I matter. "Like I'm your moon." A shadow falls over half his face. That seems to be the way of him—one toe in the shadow and one in the light.

I straighten his vest, loving the feel of the expensive material. "Why don't you let other people see this side of you? It's lovely. You're lovely."

He chuckles, shooting me a shot of his fangs when he grins. "I suppose I don't think the world is ready for me. But you seem up for any challenge, so I guess I don't bother questioning if being me will scare you away."

He holds my hand and draws it out to the side as his arm wraps around to find the small of my back. He hums a tune I don't know, his hips brushing mine as he turns me in a slow dance.

I sway in his arms with a smile that always finds me when he's near. "So, what are you going to do once you're not responsible for Drexdenberg any longer? More dancing?"

"Loads more dancing, yes." The corner of Ronin's

mouth drags upward. "I think I'll find something to occupy my time." Then his eyes soften with genuine emotion—something he doesn't let most people see. He trusts me with the glimpses of his true self, so I store them in my heart for safekeeping. "Perhaps I'll get the chance to find out who I am without the crown. I'm not sure I remember that far back."

"I'll be there while you figure it out," I promise. And I truly mean it. I want to hold onto this friend for as long as life will let me, so neither of us has to weather destiny alone.

He kisses my forehead—a quick peck meant to be traded only between lifelong friends. "And I'll be here to remind you who you are when the crown starts to make you forget. Your loves will always find you, sure, but I will never lose you."

Des throws up his arms in exasperation as he rounds the corner. "See? That right there. That's the kind of talk I don't need to hear. Get your own wife."

I snigger up at Ronin, who smirks at our innocent flirtation. I'm fairly certain he mostly does it to get under Des' skin. Ronin kisses my cheek and then stops the dance, bowing to me while I curtsy, like it's all some grand moment. Maybe it is, this turning point of the world and its leaders. Maybe in the morning, everything will look different and strange.

Ronin takes his leave while Des, Lexi and Salem migrate toward me, looking out at the window to see what I'm staring at.

"What is it? Something prowling around out there?" Salem asks, his hackles perpetually raised.

Des shakes his head. "We need more guards around here."

Lexi eyes the grounds. "The grass is too thin. It's bothering you. I can feel it. I'll go fix it now."

I touch each of them, shaking my head with a tired smile. I don't know how I got so lucky that they care so much about all the small things I don't notice. How can I when the moon is whispering promises to me that I need to hear?

"Nothing's wrong," I promise. "Maybe it won't last more than a few minutes, but I don't care. I'll take it. I'll treasure all the moments where nothing's wrong." I point to the giant sphere, my heart settling with a peace that feels permanent. "Look. It's our one perfect thing."

We stand just like that for several minutes, letting nature calm the disquiet that's always waiting to be stirred. Salem breaks the stillness first, moving to the opposite wall and sitting down with his back propped against it, motioning for me to join him.

I lower myself to sit between his knees, shivering from the slight chill emanating from the wood floor. Des and Lexi sit on either side, and for the span of a moment, the four of us gaze out the window up at the moon, believing in the hope that one day, there will be only this, and no chaos that could pull us from it.

I lean back into Salem's chest, looping my littlest finger through Des', while Lexi trills his fingers slowly up and down my forearm. Maybe life isn't perfect, but now that I'm breathing in the hope-soaked air with the people I love, it feels like this might be all I need.

Vengeful King, book 4 in the Territorial Mates series, is available now. It follows Ronin as he figures out what to do with his life after retirement from the throne.

He's plenty sexy in Book 4, and wears a selection of suits that are too beautiful for words.
You're welcome.

Here's a free preview of Vengeful King:

VENGEFUL KING

BOOK FOUR IN THE TERRITORIAL MATES
SERIES

MEANINGLESS

RONIN

I thought I would enjoy retirement more than this. I was counting on an endless stream of parties filling my nights with so much cheer that a lonely moment would never find me.

Perhaps I'm going about these affairs all wrong. I tried doubling the liquor, but I'm still watching the people toasting and laughing from a distance, never quite belonging in the place I put myself. Even the seedier elements I allowed into the affair aren't doing their part to pique my interest, though everyone else seems to be enjoying the ensuing debauchery.

Am I getting too old for this? Did I miss my prime completely? Ruling Drexdenberg for a century wasn't supposed to suck the play out of me, but I fear that's exactly what must've happened.

The band is far too loud.

The ballroom holds a mix of three kinds of people: those tweaked nearly out of their mind with wide eyes and loud voices, banging into everyone and everything without caring about where or who they are, then those on the verge of too drunk to hold more than a few sentences of lethargic conversation, and finally there are those here to simply dance.

The elaborate crystal chandelier shines on them all, each candle and bulb reflecting on the mirror-lined walls to brighten the place that still manages to feel gloomy, though, perhaps only to me. Everyone else seems to be enjoying themselves. I throw a brilliant party; I've just skipped the lesson on how to enjoy it.

And then there's me, sitting in my leather chair of importance in the corner. I had my favorite chair moved in because the brown leather is soft and the seat comfortable, even though I'm sure the setup makes me look old. It makes me feel like the king I used to be, surveying the merriment but unenthused at the prospect of being part of it.

I don't remember doing so little at parties. Then again, I've mostly attended affairs for political purposes. Shaking hands and engaging in thinly-veiled threats took up my time. Now that I've passed down the crown to my great-grandson, it's my turn to attend a party for all the normal reasons people dress up and come to these things.

Fun. Socializing. General merriment.

It's dreadful, no matter how I dress it up.

Perhaps I am a bit out of touch.

The swing band has been playing for six hours.

I was hoping this thing would go three hours and fizzle out, but apparently I'm adept at throwing parties, just wretched at enjoying them.

If I hear one more jaunty tune about vampire life being raucous and amazing, I'm going to cut the band's tip in half. Life has been anything but, yet the joyous songs keep on coming. Haven't they been paying attention?

Uniting the three territories by force wasn't the easiest thing to do, and no one was ready for the massive change. They needed the good medicine of unification, of course, but children often whine over the smallest of things, and this was no small thing.

It involved the three princes from the warring territories to all agree to marry one woman—who luckily turned out to be one of the best people I've ever known.

Still, the vampire, shifter and fae categorically stick to their own sides, even though now they're technically united under their new fae queen. It's been a year since Lilya stepped into the crown, but actual integration of the territories is remarkably slow.

"Oh, the lives we live while the others die away.

To be the ones with futures bright while the dogs and fae all fade."

. . .

I CRINGE at the lyrics being sung under my roof.

Benny's doing his laps and stops near my chair, straightening his black suit. "You look like you've sucked on a lemon. This is a party, if you didn't notice."

I sigh to my oldest friend, the head of my security. "The whole point of uniting the three territories was so the world could move forward. Songs like these that make us seem like the only race that matters feels like a giant step back, and not something a retired king should be promoting."

"Absolutely. I'll talk to them."

Benny's off in the direction of the band, conveying my wishes while keeping an eye on anyone coming too near my chair. He's good like that—keeping watch over my safety and my sanity at the same time.

A buxom beauty with too much mischief in her grin giggles at me as she crooks her finger from the dance floor. "King Ronin, you're looking lonely over there. Come on out and show us how it's done!"

As if I want to dance with her, who can't be more than twenty years old. Though everyone filling the grand hall of the royal mansion looks to be in their twenties, I've always had a knack for spotting the truly young ones, versus the young at heart.

I was frozen at age thirty-one over a century ago, but after months of throwing these grand parties only to end up watching from my leather chair in the corner, I'm starting to wonder if I was ever truly young at heart, or if I skipped that phase altogether, sacrificing carefree smiles to the doldrums of adulthood.

I dip my head graciously in the direction of the woman, but make no move to join her.

My raven-haired regular saunters to my side with a drink in her hand. "Good boy. Dancing with that young piece when you won't even take me out on the floor will only make me jealous."

I take the tumbler from her red fingernails and down half the glass in one go. Her eyebrows have been darkened and shaped to exaggerate the arch, which makes her look perpetually displeased. Though, after sleeping with her for five weeks, I'm positive that's just her normal disposition, eyebrow-sculpting or not.

"Mia, your jealousy is most unflattering. I don't dance. It's unbecoming for a ruler to be that jovial when there's been no territory-wide victory. I've thrown the party, but I don't even know what we're celebrating."

She rolls her eyes, as if I've said something vexing. As if I've no clue how to have a good time.

She may be right about that.

I'm tired of it all. It's meaningless, the whole thing. I want something real, something that matters.

"You throw parties you don't actually want to be at. *That's* what's unbecoming." Mia fluffs her breasts and smooths her silky hair that's fastened in a pearl clip I bought her.

That's one of the ways I know she was frozen a few

decades ago. Though she looks to be twenty-two, she's checking her posture and making sure the blokes in the gold-trimmed ballroom are glancing her way. She loves being seen, so much the more if she's spotted on my arm.

Meaningless, all of it.

"Go ahead and dance, Mia. I'm sure any of the blokes would love the chance to take you for a spin."

Please, take her for a spin. I'm tired of the slow drip from her subtle needling, asking for more trinkets that never satisfy. More of my attention when I'm positive she only likes being near me for my money.

Lilya encouraged me to find myself a companion. Perhaps I should've searched for more than someone who looks smashing in a tight dress and doesn't hesitate to take it off for me.

Her red fingernails trill up my forearm. "I was thinking a few of my friends could stay over tonight in one of your guestrooms. They're dying to see your collection of gold statues."

"Not tonight. I'm going to close down the party in a few, so if you wanted to get in a dance, I suggest you get on out there."

She blinks at the bulbs in the chandelier overhead. "It's too bright in here."

Yet another superfluous complaint.

I've no desire to adjust my life to suit her whims. "I prefer it this way. Enjoy the last of the party, Mia."

One of the perks of integrating the fae and shifters with

the vampires is that Prince Alexavier and Queen Lilya stay for long stretches in my mansion. Having a couple of fae around means I now have access to electricity—a novel feature in Drexdenberg. Everyone else is too wary to let a fae into their home, so they live by lamplight.

Fine by me. Let them live in the dark, for all I care. Let them watch the dancing brightness of the mansion from afar while they cling to their prejudices.

Mia scoffs and finishes her champagne. "You're no fun."

"Indeed. I'm even less fun than I was the last time you invited your friends over and one of my gold vases went mysteriously missing."

Mia avoids my eyes. It's a game we play, in which she or one of her friends sneaks something from my mansion, and I pretend not to notice because she's still putting out. It's cheaper than bedding a prostitute, though not by much, and far less scandalous on my part.

Mia slides her fingernails over my wrist. Perhaps she's trying to be seductive? I honestly can't tell anymore. "You think my friends stole something from you? You suspect your own kind when you house the fae queen? You know how tricky the fae can be." She flips her black hair over her shoulder. "That's some logic, sexy."

I loathe when she calls me that. It's like she's peeing all over me, when I made it clear I cannot be claimed.

Perhaps I've let things go on too long.

I move my hand from hers and unfasten my navy and cream striped bowtie, letting the ends dangle.

"You'll not speak like that in my home, Mia. You know I don't condone hate speech. Our queen deserves your respect, not your cattiness. There is no finer person than Queen Lilya—fae, shifter or vampire."

It's the only dance we do that actually makes me smile. I remind Mia that she's now subject to a fae woman, and she flattens her red lips to keep from rattling off her true hatred of my great-grandson's wife.

Destino knows exactly how fortunate he is to have Lilya on his arm—the very first vampire and fae union. It's only a matter of time before the rest of the world adores her in the same way.

Mia exhales loudly. "Whatever. It's not my mates who took your crummy old vase. My guess would be the shifter trash serving drinks at the bar over there. She looks hard up for cash, and she barely speaks at all. Very suspicious." She tugs at my sleeve to straighten my cuff.

I glance in the direction Mia aims her accusation, unsurprised to find someone not of our kind behind the bar. I make it a point to hire as many non-vampires as possible for my social affairs, since no one else in Drexdenberg will give them work.

Only one shifter took me up on my offer. The shifter bartender is working far too hard for a crowd who will never appreciate the effort from an outsider.

Shifters by nature aren't as kempt as vampires or fae, but the woman mixing drinks by no means looks trashy. Her auburn hair is pulled into a ponytail that curls gently at the tips. The waves brush her neck as she turns this way and that, keeping up with the line as best she can without verbally responding to a single thing anyone says. Though it's clear she's trying to fade into the background, all vampires are olive-skinned, and she is sun-kissed, sporting the expected tanned complexion all shifters are born with.

Though her standard white waitstaff tuxedo shirt is buttoned up to the throat, I know why Mia dislikes her so. It's got more to do with the bartender's generous bra size than her shifter genetics.

"Are you jealous of shifters now?" I tease, tsking Mia as I finish my drink.

She scoffs and saunters away, making sure to exaggerate the sway of her hips, which I'll admit, is a good trick. Draws my eyes easily away from the overwhelmed shifter.

Poor thing. The line of buzzards in need of a drink doesn't get any smaller, no matter how quickly she pours and mixes. She gives polite but tight smiles, nods a lot in short bursts, and keeps her eyes averted. She's trying to be as invisible as possible, braving a roomful of vampires for a paycheck she must desperately need, if she's subjecting herself to their constant disapproval and snide comments.

When the man she's waiting on starts gesturing emphatically, his head swiveling with attitude I can tell this girl doesn't deserve, something tightens in my stomach. Even though she's clearly being harassed, her lips remain locked tight, holding back any inkling to speak up for herself.

Smart girl, though the sight makes me sad.

"I'm over you dating Mia," says the only voice that

manages to coax a genuine smile from me these days. "When I suggested you find someone to spend your time with, I meant the opposite of her."

I sit up in my brown leather chair, leaning in to the touch I look forward to when her slender fingers brush my elbow. "Lilya, my love, to what do I owe the pleasure? Have you finally decided to join me at one of my parties? I've only invited you dozens of times, but you always manage to be busy. Come, enjoy what's left of the night with me. I hear my events are fabulous."

Her pale, dainty hand slides into mine, so I kiss it. "That's the thing about being queen. Not a lot of time for parties. Plus, they don't want me here. Let them have their fun." She leans forward and aims her finger in the direction of the spot next to the bar where a group of miscreants are growing increasingly rambunctious. "Are they okay?"

"I'm sure they will be someday. For now, they're young. Perhaps younger than they should be."

"Hmm." Lilya's wearing the maroon cloak I got her, the hood up and her lavender curls tucked into the velvet. I understand why she hides who she is, but it hardens off any softness to my smile. The fae are so pale, they nearly glow. There's precious little Lilya can do to blend in to a crowd, so she's taken to wearing her cloak indoors to cover hear more noticeable features.

"Come, have a drink. We've got what I'm told are the best drinks one can procure anywhere. Forget your troubles for a night, love. Be reckless with me." It's the first time I've felt like joining in on any of my lighthearted events.

She chuckles airily, knowing I'm less than half-joking. "You are trouble, that's for sure. As much as I'm thrilled at the prospect of getting stinking drunk with you, I'll pass."

I stand, pulling myself up so I can do as I please and wrap her in my arms. It's the only time I've unstuck my backside from my chair tonight.

I adore the way she molds to me so effortlessly. In another life, perhaps I would've found her first and been bewitched by her moxie before my great-grandson. But things landed how they did, and I'm okay with it.

That doesn't stop me adoring her from afar, and however close she'll allow me. In a sea of people who bow and admire my position, she's the only one who truly loves me, wicked man that I am.

I fill my lungs with the peach and lily scent of her. "I've missed you, Lilya."

She toys with the ends of my bowtie. "I was only away a couple weeks."

"Are you trying to convince me you didn't pine for me while you were away?"

"I would never tell such a filthy lie." The corner of her mouth curves, my beautiful little strumpet, but it falls just as quickly when shouting comes from the dance floor.

Though Lilya's proven she needs no backup in a fight, public brawling is for common folk, which my queen is not. So I sit her down in my chair of importance and stroll onto the dance floor, motioning to the guards at the exits to meet me at the source of the commotion.

Benny beelines for me, my head of security the first to come to my aid, as always.

A shoving match between two blokes. How droll.

"Don't touch me, man!" One of them hollers like a drunken buffoon.

The other tackles the poor bloke to the ground, though by the time Benny pulls him off his friend, he's torn a clump of hair clean off the man's head.

Meaningless, all of it. There's no honor anywhere I look.

I nod to Benny, who never hesitates to do as he's asked. All muscle and no questions—my favorite kind of guard.

Benny's short brown hair never dares to move out of place, even as he's wrestling the civilian who's high as a kite out of the mansion.

The crazed man starts screaming so high-pitched that I can't help my flinch. On his way to the exit, his leg flings out and kicks over the stand next to the bar.

I cringe when a tall stack of dozens of highball glasses flies through the air and then shatters too close to the shifter bartender, who lets out a tiny shriek at the damage.

"Enough," Benny scolds the man, and finally manages to drag him out of the ballroom.

I lift my chin to the band, my voice carrying easily, now that the music has stopped. Everyone has ceased dancing so they can drink in the hullabaloo to use as fodder for the gossip mill tomorrow. "It's an hour till sunrise. You should all make your way home."

When the band begins to play slower, softer music for people to murmur their goodbyes, too many of them linger. My fists clench, and I worry, as I often do these days, if I've lost my touch—that intangible quality that drives fear into the hearts of anyone who might consider treating my commands as mere requests.

Then I hear the gasps as worry splinters out in all directions. Of course, they're not looking at me warily, but at a figure that glides in my direction.

"Lilya, don't..." But it's no use. Her damned bleeding heart carries her feet toward the shifter bartender who's now wading in a sea of broken glass.

My darling's maroon hood is finally pulled back, so everyone stares at the scandal of her presence. Though she's been their princess for a year, and their queen for nearly half a year, the whispers and heads bowing instead of whole bodies taking a knee hits me at just the wrong angle.

The only person on their knees is the shifter bartender. I'm ashamed of my people, and it sharpens my tone when a directive belts out like the crack of a whip. "Are you all too daft to remember what you're to do when your ruler enters a room? If I have to remind my citizens to bow to their queen, perhaps I shall cut your legs off at the knee, so you'll always be showing Queen Lilya the proper respect!"

Lilya angles her chin over her shoulder to glower at me before she reaches the bar.

I don't care. She might not demand they respect her, but I will make certain of it. I handed the Drexdenberg throne down to her and Destino; I will not see it slighted.

They don't bow as one, but fall in pockets of grudging obeisance that I truly believe will one day be genuine admiration.

How could anyone not adore her?

I have to swallow the panic in my voice when Lilya descends to her knees beside the bar, picking up shards of glass because she can't help herself. It's the curse of being a good person.

I trot over to her when the people start rising and making their way to the exit. I try to keep my tone light and quiet through gritted teeth. "My queen, what do you think you're doing?"

"A freaking tap dance," she answers with no polish. The fae cadence is nowhere near as proper as the vampires'. "Want to grab a broom or something?"

I motion to my dark green suit and pull open the jacket to display the navy silk lining. "Do I look like I know where the broom is?"

She glances up at me only to narrow one eye. "What brand is that suit? Pretentious Ass?"

I pretend to peek at the label on my collar. "Why, I believe it is. Honestly, Lilya, get off the floor."

"Can you ask one of your guards to get a broom?"

"They're your guards as well, darling." I sigh, reminding myself that one day, the people will accept her as their queen, even though she's of a different race. Perhaps soon after that, she will accept that she's more important than she currently views herself.

Humility is supposedly a virtue, but I've never had much use for it.

Lilya tucks a lavender curl behind her ear. "Yes, but Benny's the only one who actually listens to me as if he doesn't hate the sound of my voice, and he's just gone outside. Please?"

I click my fingers, and a guard takes my request for a broom, returning two minutes later with the thing. The ballroom is more than half empty now, but Mia is gathering her friends with her throaty laugh that I found interesting four weeks and six days ago. At four weeks and five days, I realized my error.

I need to rectify my poor judgment and end things.

The people are leaving in droves now, unwilling to be anywhere near the queen. I chide myself for not having her remove her hood earlier. That would've cleared the room far quicker.

"Your majesty, no!" The tightlipped bartender whispers, still on her knees, her hands pressed to the floor behind the counter, bowing in the custom of the shifters. "I'll clean tha up. Ye don't need to worry about it." Her voice is sweet and bell-like, and she sounds honestly afraid of letting the queen do common chores.

On principle, I respect anyone who reveres my queen. This shifter just made my short list of people I can tolerate. She has honor in her, which makes her stand out to me.

I grab up one of the few glasses left on the countertop

and pour myself a gin and tonic. "Best of luck, getting our queen to behave like one. Though I appreciate the effort."

The shifter woman looks to be maybe twenty-seven or so. When she stands, Lilya shrieks.

The sound of panic on my queen's voice brings me to full attention, my gaze whipping to where Lilya's focusing her horror, which is the shifter's palms.

"You're bleeding! Oh, you knelt in the glass when you were bowing to me? Why did you do that? You didn't have to."

I gape at the shifter as the scent of rust enters my nose. Vampires only feed off the filtered blood of the fae, which has real flavor to it. Shifter blood is straight rust and holds no appeal nor nutritional value.

The shifter flinches as she shakes the glass from her black slacks. "I wouldn't dream of not bowing to Prince Salem's wife. You're my queen."

And just like that, I'm endeared to this woman and her reddish curls. She gets it. She understands that unity matters, that thriving involves coming together, even when it might be difficult.

She knows that progress is more important than prejudice, which is a mind I can respect.

It's the first time I've actually wanted to be at this party I've thrown.

It's the first time I've found any meaning at all in these affairs in quite some time.

I stare at the shifter, transfixed, as every guest I've invited to the party fades into the background.

Suddenly, I'm hyper-focused on this shifter.

This woman.

ORDER *VENGEFUL KING* NOW!

CHECK *in at* www.maryetwomey.com *for updates on the release of more of your favorite books.*